DEAD RINGER

By Louis Lento

DEAD RINGER

Is

Dedicated

To the one person
who allowed me to
fulfill a dream

Mary T.

CHAPTER 1

When I was growing up I loved the drive to the Cascades in the mountains. My sister and I would play games. We would count billboards. We would count the makes of cars. I was a Chevy man and she took the Fords. She always lost that one. The winner got cokes. It was a fun place to go when I was a teen-ager, lots of cool hotels and resorts where you could get drunk, laid and not worry about a damn thing, except when to go back to school. Those good 'ol days seem like a lifetime ago.

Allow me to introduce myself before I begin sharing my story with you. I'm Sal Domino, an investigator for the NGPA, the National Gambling Protective Agency. Our offices are in New York City and our goal is to protect the consumer from illegal scams on horse betting. We do our best, but some of these scams take time to unravel because they are complicated.

Nowadays you can place a bet on anything, anywhere. You can gamble on-track, off-track, bookies, Internet, from the TV and over the phone. And with technology today it, doesn't take a genius to fix a race and make a decent score. Score is gambling slang for a lot of cash, green, moola, flow, money. When things get bad I'm called in to fix the fix.

The drive to the Cascades is about three hours from the city, plenty of time to listen to the tape of the case I have been given. I'll get there just before dark.

The drive is peaceful. As I cross the George Washington Bridge on my way to Bedford, situated on the north side of the Cascades towards the middle of the state, I am reminded of the way things were. I reminisce about the trips up here when I was a kid. Families from the city would trek up to the Cascades on the weekends and summers to get away from the grind. My dad brought us there every weekend during the summers. I loved those summers, lots of great memories.

There is a little Harness Track called "Wildwood Racetrack" and I would bet a few bucks on some nag whose name I thought was neat. Of course I couldn't bet, but my Dad covered me. Wildwood used to be a hot spot about thirty years ago. It is not seeing its best days now. A conspiracy of race fixers have infiltrated Wildwood and have created havoc for everyone at the track. I've returned to Bedford to fix the mess, but this is not going to be an easy case.

I work by myself, because I think better that way. I have learned that you have to get into the mind of a criminal to catch one. I'm no crook, but I can't be completely scrupulous when I'm dealing with criminals. It helps me better understand how these guys think. They don't have a conscience and the range of criminals varies. This case includes murders, so there is more to it than just race fixing.

Darkness is approaching when I spot the inn at the Cascades on the right side of the road. Mary, my secretary, called to reserve a room for me. I pull in and get to the office quickly. These people don't work past dark up here; it's a small mountain town. An elderly woman takes my registration information and I sign in. I use an alias when I'm on a case because I learned a long time ago that I am not welcome at these tracks if they know whom I am.

I pull my Chevy around to the left side of the building, right in front of room 21. The agency won't let me have a company car anymore because I abused the cars in the past. I don't have an easy job, and I sure don't deal with altar boys either. So I use my own car, I like my Chevy.

I get out of the car with my bag. There is a thirty-eight under my jacket. I have a permit to carry it. You never know what comes with darkness. I know that I will have to watch my ass in this town, because these boys don't screw around. When it comes to greed and money lives are always expendable.

The key works. The room smells musty-stale beer and cigarettes. That's okay, because I'm going to add to the smell anyway.

As soon as I get in I call Mary on my cell phone to check in.

"Mr. Domino's office. This is Mary. How can I help you?"

"Gee, you sound so formal, loosen up a bit"

"You jerk!" Why didn't you tell me when you were leaving? They have been looking for you for three hours," she yells.

"Easy now, honey. I didn't want to talk to anyone because they are going to stick me with a punk intern, and you know I don't like that, so I scooted. I'm sorry. I should have left you a note."

"I covered your slimy ass again. Did you find the inn okay?"

"Yeah, it was a nice drive, it brought back good memories. The leaves are turning, maybe you should plan on coming up for awhile to help with the case."

" I've got plans!"

"You always have plans, but they never include me."

"Maybe next time-you be careful. There were two murders up there. These guys play rough. Call me if you need anything".

"Thanks"

Mary and I used to have a thing for each other some time back. She gave up on me because I can be such a jerk. I'm stuck on my bad habits of drinking and smoking, but I'm also still stuck on her, and she knows it. Maybe later on down the road--I keep on hoping.

I am hungry and thirsty so I and my thirty-eight head across the street to a 24-hour store. It's easy to forget all the problems you have after a couple of brewskis and a few cigs.

I walk back across the street to the inn. As I approach my room I get an uneasy feeling. You get that way after seventeen years as an investigator. As a precaution I have made it a habit to put transparent tape over the doorjamb when I leave a room. I have been jumped a few times over the years and tonight my experience pays off. The tape is flapping; someone has been in my room.

The thirty-eight is in my hand in a flash. I check the lock. The door is unlocked. I know that I locked it when I left. I step to the side, turn the knob and gently push the door open as I stay out of a possible line of fire. I wait what seems like an hour, but it is only a minute or so. I don't hear anything so I reach in and turn on the light switch. No action--I walk in carefully.

My clothes are strewn all over the room. Someone was in a hurry and obviously didn't find what they were looking for. I search the rest of the room, including the bathroom. There is no sign of forced entry, so I am guessing it was a pro, or maybe that little old lady at the desk isn't so nice and cute after all. I have nothing of value in my bag and I always carry my ID on me.

Who could know I was on my way to the Cascades? The order came from Jack Lindsey, the man in charge of the national task force. The orders always come in a sealed envelope and Mary is the only other person to read them. If I eliminate those two people, there must be a leak somewhere, but where? I don't have any friends in the Agency. I have pissed off way too many people! That is one reason I work alone. Who would know that I arrived?

I don't trust anyone, and if I'm going to take a bullet, then I want all the blame to fall on me. I don't want to be responsible for anyone else. Selfish? Damn straight. I'm still alive and I intend to stay that way.

Before I go to the track tomorrow I will have to be careful

and pay more attention. The people who know I'm here know my real name and for whom I work. The alias I am using will not fly with these jerks. I need another cig and brew. Damn! Why are people screwin' with me already? I just got here. Did they know about the case before I did? After a few more brews I finally fall asleep.

CHAPTER TWO

I wake up with a hangover, a few too many brewskis.
Tough shit, it's my headache. After a shower I get dressed and
walk across the street to the 24-hour store. Before I leave the
room I put tape on the door again. I don't expect any trouble,
but you never know. The thirty-eight is comfortably tucked in
the shoulder holster, out of sight. The coffee tastes great.
Coffee is always the remedy for all ailments. I sip the coffee
slowly and think of my plan.

The reason I am called in on this case is because the bets
that were made have crossed state lines. The state boys are
kept out of it. They will still be snooping around, but when
they see me they know that the feds are in charge. Most of the
states treat me okay, with just a few exceptions. New York is
one of the good guys, because there are a lot of retired NYC
cops on their force. A good bunch of guys, I can count on
them if I get in a jam.

I decide to jump in the Chevy and drive the ten miles to
the track. The traffic is pretty thin for a Friday. My cover is
probably already blown. I have most of the morning and afternoon to snoop around because there will only be nighttime
racing today.

As I make my way towards the main building I look at the
parking slots and spot a name I am familiar with, Bill Beane.
Bill is the Security chief at Wildwood and will be very helpful
to me. He's an ex-state trooper and a no-nonsense guy who is
very efficient. I know he is angry about this case happening in
his own backyard. Nobody wants trouble on his or her own
turf.

I park in the visitors' area and check my thirty-eight. I get out of the car and look around. The track is going through tough times. The parking lot needs to be paved, the building needs paint, and no telling how bad the backstretch is.

As I walk towards the main building I can see the track. It is busy this morning with horses and drivers going through their morning exercises. The smell of manure, sweat, straw, and oats, brings back good memories from my childhood. Unfortunately, this visit will not be a pleasant one.

I walk along the first floor in hopes of seeing a security office. I get lucky.

"Hello. I'm looking for Bill Beane. Is he around?" I ask.

A grumpy old fellow snarls at me.

"What do you want him for?" shouts the old coot.

I make up a story.

"Bill and I were in the State Troopers together. I was driving by so I thought I would stop in and say hi."

The old coot smiles. "Well, you're in luck. I'll find him for you. Base to one, come in one," screeches the inter-com.

"Go ahead base."

"Someone here to see you, boss, says he's a friend of yours," says the old timer.

"I'll be right there. I'm in the backstretch," answers Bill.

I thank the old timer and walk outside to smoke a cigarette.

After walking the first floor waiting for Bill I notice that the interior needs paint too. Rough times all right. I hear voices. Bill is approaching with a real dirt-bag looking guy. Bill is chewing him out for smoking in a barn. Fires can start easily if you're careless. I wait until he is done with the chew.

"Well, I'll be damned," shouts Bill. " I heard you were coming. I would tell you I am happy to see you Sal, but that would be a lie. I know why you are here."

"It's always good to see you Bill. Unfortunately, I am not here for a vacation. Is there someplace we can talk?"

"Let's jump in the car and take a spin," reasons Bill.

We walk to the car that is parked in his slot. Bill always likes to run around in a beater, he can't stand to dirty his good car at a racetrack. Besides, Ellie, his wife of 37 years won't let him drive the Caddy anyway. I can tell he is upset.

" Do you want to tell me about it Bill?"

"Sal, these guys are real pros, they got a real fixing ring going on. We aren't the only track to get stung. As a matter of fact, the word is there is a lady involved, and she is running the show. I can't prove it, but one of my informants here at the track told me he heard some talk at the track kitchen one morning. That was shortly after the second murder. I'll tell you what I know, and we'll go from there."

Bill talks very slowly so I can digest what he's saying. I have been involved in a lot of racetrack scams over my seventeen years, but the story he is telling seems right from an action film.

It was a Wednesday evening race card when the conspirators chose to put their scam in effect. There aren't a lot of bettors attending Wednesday race cards, but the ones that are there bet with both fists. It seems the whole nation bets on Wildwood, so the pools are enormous. Of course, the people at the track have a huge advantage over the people that bet off the track, including over the Internet, TVs, phones and every other available way to wager.

The ninth race of the ten-race-card included a full field of eight horses, cheap claimers. Some are so bad on paper, that it's amazing people actually put money on them. There are a few favorites, but the majority of the entrants are nags. The betting pools are enormous. Millions of dollars are being bet. Bill makes it a habit to watch everything very closely. He had a bad feeling about this race from the beginning.

When he glanced at the trifecta pool, there is a larger total of money than normal. The pool is so large that the race had to be held up to allow for all of the money bet on the combinations that were bet nationally to get in on the betting pool.

The money wasn't coming from on-track patrons, but off-track. The race had to start four minutes late to get things straight. He noted on the tote board that $2,542,108 is bet in that trifecta pool!

As the race unfolds horses and their drivers take their positions on the track. This is not unusual, but what happened next is. The even-money horse broke stride around the second turn and had to be pulled up. The race continued without incident until the stretch run. The second favorite is tucked along the rail and did not have any racing room. Sort of like, 'hey, I got a lot of horse, let me through' type thing. Well, a few horses and drivers did not allow that horse to 'get through'. The race concluded, with the first three finishers being long shots. The few patrons who were at the track went crazy. The prices were going to be off the charts. No one could have picked those horses, 1-2-3! It's impossible. The race was made official.

When you pick three horses to finish 1-2-3 that is a trifecta. That bet has been around for years. It's pretty damn hard to pick horses to finish exactly 1-2-3. Bill is alert. After spending all those years in the State Troopers, he comes to expect the unexpected. There was a delay in posting the prices. After several minutes, the natives were beginning to get restless. Bill notified his staff to watch for any trouble. He sort of anticipated what was going to happen. The prices were posted on the tote board. He knows what should happen and not happen at a racetrack.

The five years he has spent at Wildwood, for the most part, have been enjoyable. He has had a few problems with thieves and drugs, but normally everything has been running okay-up until now. Here are the results of that race and the prices to be paid out: win, place, show and trifecta.

8 - Jumpin'Jimmy	$242.80	$97.20	$38.00
4 - Loose Girl		$87.40	$51.60
5 - Grab a Sac Ful			$67.00

The 8-4-5 trifecta price with all these longshots is
$217.60. However, there was something drastically wrong.
Win, place and show betting pools are separate from the trifecta pools, but usually there is a similarity in the betting pattern. Not this time. Although there were only about a thousand
people at the track, these people became irate. They boo the
drivers, the judges, security and everyone else within shouting
distance. They proceeded to pile benches on top of on another.
One guy took his lighter and emptied the fluid onto the benches and started a fire. The place was in total chaos! Bill immediately dispatched his staff to the fire. He also called for
County Sheriff backup.

The remaining race that evening had to be cancelled.
Several people were arrested, including one lady who went up
to the general offices and tried to beat the shit out of the
General Manager. What a fiasco! It seems that lady had the
winning combination. It was the age of her kids, and she
played it every trifecta. She figured that the price of the trifecta should have been several times larger than the price that
was posted. Little did she know she would be right.

It took Bill and the sheriff's office two hours to get everything in order. He called Ellie and told her not to keep a late
supper for him. He had a major problem at hand and was
needed at the track. Ellie had learned not to question him anymore. After thirty years with the troopers there were nights
when he never arrived home. She just hoped he was alive
when he did get home. Bill wrapped up his paperwork around
3:00 a.m. and finally went home.

I am very patient with Bill as he continues with the
details of the story. He is sorting through his thoughts so as
not to miss anything. I told you he is a very efficient cop. He

starts again.

Exercising horses starts very early at a racetrack, as early as 5:00 a.m. Grooms, trainers and drivers are out trying to find the right combination to their horse. Wildwood is considered a cheap track and these people have to work doubly hard to find that elusive combination. Most of these track people are hard working dedicated workers, working for peanuts. Most of them have a passion for training these animals and get tremendous joy out of the work that they do. However, there is always a criminal element that spoils it for the honest ones just trying to make a living and enjoying the work that they do.

The following day Bill knew he would be in for a long and exhausting day and he arrived at the track at 6:00 a.m. Paul Olmstead, a trainer-driver, was found dead in his tack room just a few minutes before Bill got there that day. It seemed that the groom found him lying on a bale of hay. He had been stabbed several times. Blood was everywhere. Olmstead was a veteran driver and a guy who didn't mix with the track jerks.

Paul was the driver of Crystal Delight that night. Crystal Delight was the horse that 'broke' going around turn two. It is known around the backstretch that if you want to play games with the horses don't mess with Olmstead. He didn't like to play games, and he told everyone that. He was a hard working guy, a single Dad with two older boys. The boys were seen working his stable after school and on weekends.

Bill figured that Olmstead said the wrong thing to the wrong person. If Olmstead wasn't going to play along he would be eliminated, and not just from the race. Bill was shaken. Olmstead was a likeable guy, a no-nonsense guy, like he is. He felt bad for the kids.

His rover, who tours the grounds in an old Jeep, called him on the radio and told him to get over to barn J on the double. Bill jumped in his beater and drove the short distance to

16

Barn J. Jack Ballot, another ex-cop, pointed to a body on shed row. Bill noticed that Jack drove the Jeep across the entrance to the barn so as not to draw suspicion from any of the backstretch people. They would find out soon enough. Jack is perfect for the rover job. He gets along with almost everyone and has developed quite a network back there. Bill uses the network when he needs information.

Bill recognized the body; Cotton Jones laid in a twisted position in front of stall # 4, sort of in an "S". The position was not normal. Bill leaned over the body and figured Cotton's neck was broken. Cotton was the groom for Slow Poke. Slow Poke is the horse that got boxed in along the rail and couldn't 'get out.' Cotton was a lovable old black guy who had been caring for horses most of his life. He came from the bush tracks in Louisiana and got along with everyone, I mean everyone. He didn't have an enemy at the track. He drank a lot, but when he got that way, someone would give him a lift to the Grooms' building to sleep it off. He never left the grounds. His whole world was the 50-acre backstretch, that's all he needed.

Bill was puzzled. He had two dead bodies and a fixed race. Both of these men were associated with the two horses that didn't 'play along'. I listen in total amazement. His attention to detail is extraordinary. The tape I received from Jack at headquarters did not have the details of the story I'm hearing now. The scope of the crime is going to be on a national scale and the people that made the score have a lot more going on, more that just fixing races. Murder usually isn't part of trying to dupe the public out of money. Whoever was behind this scam has plenty of money and muscle.

I reflected back to last night. It is obvious to me now that I could be another victim. I realize, after listening to Bill's story, how close I came to my own demise. I have to be extra careful.

CHAPTER THREE

I thank him for the story and tell him where I'm staying. I guess that is no secret. I don't want to move, but I may have to. I gave him my cell phone number in case he thinks of anything else to tell me. Before I leave the grounds I drive around the backstretch.

Even though the barn area is pretty rundown, it is fairly neat. Horsemen take great pride in keeping a clean stable. I drive up and down the roads until I come upon the barn of Paul Olmstead. He shares the barn with two other trainer-drivers. I recognize the area, because the sheriff's office put the yellow police tape around it, designating it as a crime scene. I want to snoop around. I duck under the tape and proceed to the tack room where the body was found.

The door is open and I walk in, being careful not to touch anything. The bale of hay is still intact, and blood still evident. There is no sign of a struggle. Everything seems to be in order. This leads me to believe that Olmstead may have known his killer.

I turn to walk out when something catches my eye. The way the sun is setting, it happens to shine over the barn just at the right angle. I think I see a piece of glass or something and I go and check it out. Behind a bale of hay I see an old pair of boots. The buckle is reflecting the light from the sun. The boots look like a regular old, smelly pair of boots, until I look inside. I find a wad of bills stuffed in the toe of one of the boots. I didn't want to remove them in case prints are legible, so I take my pen and fiddle with them until they come loose.

I discover a bunch of one-hundred-dollar bills. Now what would Paul Olmstead be doing with a wad of c-notes? This guy worked hand-to-mouth, worked hard, and barely made expenses, so where did it come from? He would make extra money by training other horses, but he wouldn't make this kind of money. I estimated that there were several thousand bucks in that boot. I put the boot back exactly as I found it.

I'm sure someone will be looking for the money, probably the same people that killed him. I left quickly. As I left I looked around to see if I was noticed, but it looks okay. I didn't know then, but my every move was watched.

I don't think Olmstead is involved with the thieves, but the money, where did it come from? I carefully manage to turn around and make my way over to barn J. As with the Olmstead barn, the Sheriff neatly marked the barn with yellow tape. The ground where Cotton was found dead is still trampled over. The stalls are neat. The race department moved the other horses out of both barns until the murder cases were solved. I move around slowly, trying not to disturb anything.

The tack room is at the end of the hall; so I saunter down to take a look. The tack room is the primary location for all supplies and schedules relating to a stable. I thought I would find something just like at Olmstead's barn, but nothing. Cotton kept a neat barn. The trainer-driver that Cotton worked for, Judy Campbell, is not around. She is someone I will need to speak to, and soon. Bill said she shipped one of her horses out of town. I will catch up to her later. Nothing stirred me at this scene.

I hop back in the Chevy and find my way to the groom's building where Cotton had a room. It is a large two-story brick building, also needing paint. I park in a dirt lot on the south side of the building. I think a second, and then turn the Chevy around and back in, a survival trick I learned along the way. This is not a place I want to be stuck in if I need to escape quickly. I walk to the front door. One door is off the hinge, and the bottom glass panel is shattered. I don't envy Bill trying to watch this place. I walk gingerly down the first floor hallway.

"What you doin' in here Whitey?"

I turn around slowly. In front of me is a huge black man with hands the size of large pizzas. I can't run, 'cause he is blocking the way. Come on Sal-think quickly.

"Big fella, you scared the shit outa me."

He didn't smile or move.

"Look, I don't want any trouble. I was just looking for Cotton, he owes me some money, and I thought he was around"

"You ain't getting no money from Cotton, 'cause he's dead," says the big fella. "Now why don't you get your ass outa here afore I throw you out," he says sternly.

Sal, you need to act surprised.

"I'm sorry. Cotton was a good customer of mine. You see, I'm a bookie and Cotton played with me. I used to let him float along, 'cause he was such a swell guy. He always paid. Shit, I can always make more money. Damn, Cotton was a super guy."

The big man let his guard down a little. The tension in his face softened somewhat, but this was a dangerous man.

"You used to take book for Cotton? He used to talk all the time about this white guy that helped him out from time to time, that must be you," he grins.

Wow, talk about getting lucky! I dodged a bullet there.

"That's me. When Cotton wanted to bet the football games, he came to me." I smile. "You need action?"

The big man continues, "No way man. I drink and play the horses, that's all I can afford," he gloats. "Too bad about Cotton. They found him with his neck broke one morning, probably something to do with that damn race."

I need to play dumber then I was being.

"I heard about the race, not about the murders."

The smile vanished from his face.

"Who said anything about more than one murder." He

glares at me.

Dumbass. Now what the hell you gonna do?

"I was at the track kitchen and heard about some shit going down. I was listening what was being said. No harm big fella," I say confidently.

"You can call me Horseshoe."

Then he sticks out one of those big meat hooks of a hand. I take it. Goodness gracious, his hand entirely covers mine. I'm no small guy, but this man is huge. His shake is firm, but not offensive, but it could be, anytime he wants it to be. I surmise he has something to do with the shoeing of horses. I know one thing; I need to get on this man's good side. I feel sorry for the person who is on the other side.

"Besides being a groom, I shoe horses on the side. The track blacksmiths rob these people blind and I don't charge nearly as much and do a better job," he crowed.

"Nice to meet you Horseshoe, but I gotta go. If you decide to change your mind about the football, I'll find you."

"Thanks, but no thanks. Hey, I didn't get your name," he says.

"Just call me bookie, I'll be around." I walk away, swiftly.

I knew there was a reason why I back into parking slots; I almost needed it that time.

I drive out the rear guard gate. The guard and I make eye contact. Bill has already alerted his men. There is no wave or talk. Ex-cops know what is going on and I feel very safe.

I drive back to the inn. The ten miles seem to go by fast. I have a lot on my mind. I am lucky enough to spot a silver Caddy that is changing lanes as I am. I decide to take a detour, even though I don't know where the hell I'm going. I make a right turn off the highway and stop at the stop sign. I make believe I am confused as to which way to turn. I want to see what the Caddy is going to do. He is right behind me and not in any hurry. He waits me out. I turn left at the sign that reads Cascade Caves. Shit, I don't have a clue where I am; this is no place to get lost when you are being tailed. I drive a few miles. The Caddy is persistent. I pull into a seven-eleven to pick up a package of cigarettes. The Caddy drives around to the back of the store. I manage to catch a glimpse of the car as it turns in the back. The driver is a young man, with shades on. It's overcast outside, with very little chance of the sun peeping through, and this clown is wearing shades. I can't see the tag. I think my ass is in the wringer. I jump back in the Chevy and drive the same route back to the highway, the Caddy follows. It's time to shit or get off the pot. I drive to the inn and park in front of my room. The thirty-eight is getting restless and hasn't been used for a while. The Caddy stops at the office. I see the nice little old lady talking to the punk, the conversation looks innocent enough. As I approach the door something catches my eye. The tape is flapping again. Why don't these assholes shoot my dago ass and get it over with! They keep screwing with me! The punk is eyeing me, so I make like I don't notice him. I then did something I very rarely do, I open the door carelessly and walked in. That is the last thing I remember.

I wake up with a doozy of a headache. I feel my head and realize my brains are still intact, although somewhat fuzzy. The blow is nice and neat, no blood. My neck feels as if there are two of them trying to fight for position on my head. A pro. I shake the cobwebs out and look around. On the desk is a note.

"Be on your way home, or be dead, your choice. We got nothing to lose."

I have investigated gambling crimes all over the States, even abroad in England and don't scare easily. I grab a beer; at least they didn't steal that. I need to think, but that is diffi-cult right now. I pass out after guzzling the brew and wake up a few hours later.

These assholes know my every move. If I had a family they would probably be held hostage, or be dead by now.

What is it that disturbs these guys so much? Hell, I just got here and I haven't even formulated my plan, nor do I have any suspects. I feel the thirty-eight and it's still there, but anxious. The cell phone is okay. I need to call Mary. I try to get up, but have to hold the bed for a second. As I try to gain my senses, I notice an odor. That odor is familiar to me and I've smelled it before, rather recently. It smells like a cheap perfume, a rather distinct smell. I'm not thinking too clearly, ah forget it.

I look out the window to check on the Caddy. It's gone. Of course it's gone, it was a set-up and I fell for it. Someone was laying for me; an old trick and this stupid ass fell for it. I deserve a headache. I walk outside and dial Mary.

"Good morning, Sal Domino's office."

"It's me, I got a headache and I'm pissed."

"What happened, are you all right?"

Hey, maybe we are making headway here. She sounds like she cares for me again. Nah, it's got to be the headache.

"Bumped and bruised a little, nothing serious. Mary, does anyone from the agency know I'm here? My cover has been blown, and I've been tailed and roughed up a bit. Someone doesn't like my being here."

"Just me and Jack, as usual. What are you saying?"

"Some people already knew I was coming here. The welcoming committee wasn't so welcoming. I need you to back check the orders. I think we have a leak." I wait for a reply.

"Are you crazy? You know very well that me and Jack are the only two people who know your cases," she yells.

"Easy baby, you guys are the best, but someone other than you and Jack, knows something about this case. I'm being set up." I wait again, but this time the wait is a little longer.

"I don't know what to say. Nothing like this has ever happened to us before Sal. I don't know where to look," she says, concerned.

"Do the best you can Mary, and cover your tracks. You don't need to be in any more danger than you already are.

These people are playing rough and the deal is a lot larger than just this race at this rinky-dink track. We have stumbled on a major race-fixing scam that branches out nationally. From now on go to a pay phone and call me. We have to communicate outside of the office from now on. It will be safer. If you have to talk to me in an emergency, call the cell phone from the office and let it ring once, then go directly to the pay phone. We'll hook up there. I don't care where the phone is, just so it is away from the agency. You call me every day at 6:00 p.m., if I'm not dead. You got it?" I wait patiently. Mary will be involved just because she is hooked up with me.

"Yes, yes, I understand. I'm scared Sal. Suppose they kill you, and then come after me. What am I gonna do?"

I have no answer, but she needs comforting.

"Trust me, Mary. I won't let us down. I'll get these scumbags. I realize that I have to be more careful. The only person I can trust here is Bill Beane. You'll remember him if you meet him, he is the security chief, a good cop. He'll cover me, now get to work and find that leak. Talk to you later. Remember, every night at 6:00 p.m. Call me with the number when you pick out a phone. Okay?"

"Okay Sal. Be careful. Don't drink too much. You need to be sharp. I don't want to seem like I'm nagging, but I want you alive. Okay?"

Well, shit. What's a man going to say after that!

"Okay Mary. Thanks for the concern." I am drained.

It is getting late and I had a busy day, if you call getting the piss knocked out of you and being threatened with death a busy day. I do. I shower and dress. I decide to grab a bite to eat at some steak house I passed on the way to this hellhole. Maybe filling my belly will allow me to think clearer. I know my brains are jumbled up a bit but they still work. I put the usual tape on the door. I'm surprised the boys haven't seen the tape yet. I use a transparent tape, one that can barely be seen. You have to feel it to detect it. I lock the door and proceed to the Chevy. I'm not smart enough to figure out how to detect a bomb on a car. There are so many places to hide one, it would take hours to try and find one. I figured that if these assholes wanted me dead they would have knocked me off already. They have proven to me that murder doesn't bother them. If that is the case, then why are they keeping me alive?

I drive about fifteen miles to the steak house. It seems like a nice joint, on the outside. I back into a parking space because I'm not taking any chances considering what's already happened in only a day. I lock the Chevy and walk into the restaurant. The place is half full, so finding me a table won't be hard. The slicked-haired host welcomes me and asks if I have a preference. I ask for a table in the smoking section, with a window by the lake. He agrees. We walk to the window area and he finds me a cozy table. I wish Mary were here. Damn, I don't want her involved with me on this one.

A saucy little number waltzes over and asks if I need a drink. I remember what Mary said to me, but what the hell. I order a beer. I look around, nice joint, really nice. I wonder if this is a wise guy hangout? It sure has all the ingredients for one. No one caught my eye as I look around, except some dame at the bar. I notice her looking at me when I walk in. I am not overly dressed, nor am I the most handsome of guys, so I wonder why the stare. The waitress brings the brew and I tell her to bring another because this one will be gone very quickly. As I am sipping the brewski the dame walks over. I see her when she gets up; she is dressed to the hilt, nice threads and jewelry to match. I didn't notice a ring. My guess is a high-class hooker. I was soon to find out differently.

"Mind if I join you?"

Maybe this is my lucky day; I get up from my seat. I do have some manners, although Mary says I'm a chauvinist.

"Not at all, please be seated."

"Thank you. I don't recall seeing you around here before, are you passing through?"

Boy, a line right out of the movies, already I don't trust her.

"I'm here on business. I come up here often, just not to this joi---I mean establishment."

"Most people that come up here are affiliated with the track. Do you race horses?"

Aha, another setup. I play along.

"Not really, but I do follow the horses." I lie. "This is a beautiful part of the country this time of year. I enjoy the drive more than anything."

"Yes, you're correct, it is beautiful. So what brings you up on this trip?" She is persistent.

I need to be careful. I don't want to get laid, shit; I couldn't afford this tart anyway. She was sent on a fact-finding mission. I guess I'll feed her some lies.

"Actually, I do have a meeting with the management of the track about installing a new lighting system. It is a revolutionary system, with lighting that costs half as much to use. They can save a huge amount of money, and I know that they can use a little savings, they haven't been doing so well lately," I explain. I don't have a clue about a lighting system. I wouldn't know one bulb from another. I was hoping she didn't either.

"Very interesting, I suppose you heard about the murders up there?

I have to play along.

"Yeah, a real shame. There was some talk about a bad payout on a race, or something like that. I don't bet that much, so I wouldn't know if the payouts are right or wrong," I reason. She bit.

" Yes, I'm very depressed. I was very close to one of the guys that was killed."

Damn. Well it sure wasn't Cotton so it had to be Olmstead. I plug along. Maybe I've got her figured wrong. She wants to continue.

She stares at me. I must say, for a hooker she is sharp.

"You don't sell light bulbs, do you Sal?"

I am surprised, the whole damn world knows me and I don't know shit. She has me, so here goes.

"What's your angle, honey? I don't want to put up with any more than I have to in this shit hole of a town," I blurt.

"My, what happened to the gentleman a minute ago?" She says it sarcastically, and has me again.

"Sorry. Let's put it all on the table, sweetheart. My patience is wearing thin. If you've got something to say, then spit it out."

"Bill told me you were a son of a bitch, he's right," she observes. " I had to look and check you out myself. I have to make sure that you can help me. My name is Gretchen Olmstead. I'm Paul's younger sister."

I was so preoccupied trying to figure her as some whore on the make or worse yet, a honey to some big ass wise guy. I study her carefully. I didn't know Paul, just from the picture Bill showed me. I can see the resemblance. She has the same chiseled features, just a lot more refined. She really is very attractive. She has fairly rough looking hands. I guess she works with Paul and the kids at the stables. She looks me square in the eyes. I can't run. She isn't going to cry, but she is getting there. I figured wrong, and it is time to own up to that. I look right square back at her.

"I assume Bill sent you. Why didn't Bill tell me about you?"

"Bill only knows me from the barn area. I called him at home and asked to speak to him. He agreed and we met at the grocery store down the street from his house. He checked me out before we met. It satisfied him, how about you?"

"Keep going, I'll reserve judgment," I really didn't mean it.

"Bill doesn't see me much because I race a small stable of horses at a track in Pennsylvania. I ship in from time to time to race a horse at Wildwood. Paul and I have been in business for about five years. We barely make a living at this, but we continue to strive, looking for that one horse that will make us some money. Sal, I want to help you find the people that killed my brother. I will do anything you ask. Bill says you are the best there is. What do you say?" she pleads.

"Just a minute, I have to see a man about a horse. Will you excuse me?"

I find the men's room, but take a detour out the back door. I grab the cell phone and call Bill at home, Ellie answers. She gets Bill, who is working in his shed. I ask Bill about Gretchen and he verifies who she is. I thank him and tell him not to cut off his fingers until we solve the case.

She is in the same position as when I left her.

"Well, do I check out?"

I could see that I wasn't going to pull anything over on this lady.

"Gee, was I that obvious?" I laugh. That broke the ice. We both laugh. Boy, she sure is pretty. Get to the case, Domino.

"Okay, Gretchen, tell me what you know."

She continues, "Paul was an honest man, Sal. After our Daddy died we assumed the family racing business. We were never interested in racing but we helped out in the barn area and the farm. I'm a college graduate with a degree in economics. We talked it over, and decided to give racing a try. Paul would do most of the racing and I would take care of the business side. We have been doing okay, but it is a struggle. I know my brother would never get involved with those crooks. When Jill, his ex-wife, ran off and left the kids, Paul wanted the best for those boys but he would never, never cheat. Those boys meant the world to him. It's a tragedy. Oh, I want to kill those people", she yells.

People look at the table. I have to settle her down.

"Alright Gretchen, easy now. Let's get out of here."

I slap down a ten spot, wave at the waitress, and escort Gretchen out of the restaurant. I am still hungry.

We leave her truck in the parking lot and take the Chevy.

"Are you hungry?" I ask-because I am!

"A little, I guess I should eat something," she reasons. "There is a little diner just up the road, we can stop there, it's out of the way, no horsemen."

We drive into the parking lot. I pull, not back, into a slot. I feel no one will mess with me as long as a pretty lady is present. I must be getting soft.

We shuffle to a booth. A chubby waitress with a wad of gum in her mouth takes our order. We order a couple of burgers and sit quietly as we wait for them. The fries are greasy, but the burger is good. We resume our conversation over coffee.

"Gretchen, I have no leads. I just arrived yesterday, and already I have been tailed and mugged. Bill doesn't know that yet, but I'll bring him up to snuff in the morning. I know one thing for sure; my presence here has caused quite a stir. The only idea that sounds good to me is that these crooks are fixing races on a national level. With me being here, they figure I know something, which I don't -but they don't know that I don't know shit. That is the only leverage I have over them. They think I know a lot more than I do.

Do you get the picture?"

"I must tell you that these guys are playing for keeps. They left me a message that said they have nothing to lose. A few more murders won't heat up the electric chair any hotter. They'll fry no matter what the temperature. Do you understand what I am telling you?" I ask harshly. I want to shake her up a bit and see if she wants to bow out. She didn't flinch. She really is a tough and attractive girl.

She wants to pay for her half of the bill. I let her. The drive back to her truck is silent. I pull into the steakhouse lot and spot the truck. The silence is deafening. I talk a lot of trash, so I am not doing so good right now. She looks over at me.

"I mean what I say, Sal. I want to help you get these people. I will do anything you want. I'm smart and tough. I knew when I set eyes on you that I could trust you. Can I?"

Wow. That look is going to get me in trouble. Right now Mary is the farthest thing from my mind. Come on Domino-stick to the case.

"Get a good night's sleep, Gretchen, if that's possible. I will look you up at the barn area in the morning. I assume you will be caring for Paul's horses. I know the race department has moved the stable, so I'll find you. Try and keep a low profile, don't answer any questions. Play stupid. I know that will be hard for a college girl, but the less you say the better. I will inform Bill that you will be coming and that we had this conversation. Expect a shout from him. You can brief him on what we said if he gets to you before I do in the morning. Good night." I wait. I didn't know if she was going to try and kiss me, hit me, or cry. She has a poker face. None of that happened. She simply opened the door and walked to her truck. I waited to see if she fired up, she does and I leave.

I start back to the inn. The past events at the inn have made me skeptical. I hope I don't have the usual welcome this time; I just can't handle it right now. The inn is dark as I pull in front of my room. The only light on is in the office. It shows the inn is open for late visitors. Of course there is never anyone there, just a note that allows a person to ring a bell. The visitor can get lucky and get a room or hit the road. I surmise that the latter happens more often than not. I can't see that nice little old lady getting up at two in the morning to hustle forty bucks for a room.

I check the thirty-eight, he's getting grumpy. The tape is still on the door, and I don't smell anything unusual. I open the lock and walk in, the light switch works. The room has been cleaned, nice and neat. I check the bathroom. All is clear. I let down my guard, which means it's brewski time. All the brews are still in the position I left them in. At least the cleaning people don't drink on the job. My lighter still works, and I light a cig. I sit on the bed and begin to think.

Of course I didn't mention to Gretchen the money that I found in the boot. I wonder if she knew Paul had it? I'll find out in the morning. Another brew makes me groggy. My head still hurts from that whack on the neck. I fall asleep with Gretchen on my mind.

CHAPTER FOUR

It is 7:30 a.m. when I wake up, still groggy. The clown that whacked me did a hell of a job. The pain is a reminder that they don't fool around. I respect the lingering effect it gives me; although I'm pissed it happened. While I shower I try to finally come up with a plan. Knowing Gretchen, she will be tending to the stable; she's been there a couple of hours already. I better get my lazy ass going. I dress, lock the room, and put the usual tape on the door. I want to eat breakfast, but hold off for a reason. I want to eat in the track kitchen. Anything and everything can be uncovered in a track kitchen. You just have to separate the fact from the bullshit. There is more bullshit than fact. You'll hear a story about a world-beater of a horse who happens to be a $2000 claimer. A lot of bullshit, just like I said.

The rear guard gate is very busy each morning. Horsemen ship their horses to other tracks to race; feed trucks come in, along with manure wagons. Everyone has to be logged in and out. Knowing Bill the way I do, he is very meticulous about this portion of security. If it is the list on the night of the murders that may help us find who committed the murders. If everyone checks out then we have an inside job. That will really piss Bill off!

I am third in line for entrance into the barn area. Bill only has one man in the booth. He has to cover both sides, the people going in as well as the ones signing out. The man at this gate is very thorough. Since this is the only way in or out, he has to be good at what he does. No one will bullshit this guy. I drive up to where he is standing. This man is a different guy than the one last night, but he has the same look-an ex-cop.

He pretended to look at a sheet of paper and mumbled, "go ahead, Bill is waiting for you." No one could hear him, except me. Bill's office is in the main building, but he has one in the backstretch also. He does all the fingerprints and paperwork relating to horsemen back here. I recognize the old beater parked in front of a small shack and park next to it. There is no need to back in here. The shack is located near the training track, which most of the racetracks have. Nearly all of the training and exercising are done here. The main track is used only for official workouts or schooling of young horses. There is a constant bantering from the trainers as they put their steeds through the morning jogs. The activity is awesome. You wouldn't think this track is in financial trouble, but looks are deceiving.

At the entrance to the training track I spot Gretchen. She is climbing into the sulky, getting ready to work out one of Paul's pacers. She doesn't see me. Before I engage Bill I try to catch her eye so I move to the rail by the track. The track is a half-mile around, so it doesn't take her long to go by where I am standing. She looks great. She handles the horse like a pro. She strides by me, sitting tall in the sulky, and looking up. We make eye contact that is all we need. When I walk back to the shack it is apparent that Bill is watching us.

"Good morning, after I left you, I had quite an ordeal."

I fill him in on the tale and the mugging. He didn't recognize the Caddy or the hood wearing glasses. I also bring him up to snuff on the conversation with Gretchen.

" I figure you would like her. I checked her out pretty good, she's legit. Sounds as if you two got along okay. You aren't getting any ideas, are you Sal?"

"I have to admit, she's sharp." That's as far as I want to go with that. Stay focused Domino.

I ask Bill if Judy Campbell is back yet. He checks the log and notices she arrived early this morning from a track in Ohio. A long trip just to race a horse. Bill tells me she is rclocated in barn N. He points in that direction. The morning is beautiful, so I decide to hoof it. It is a pretty lengthy walk. The walk does me good, not because I need the exercise, but to analyze how Cotton got ambushed in this deal. I am hoping Judy can give me some answers. I lumber up the hill to barn N, and notice a flashy-looking Lexus parked by the barn. A long-legged woman in her thirties is washing a horse. As I stroll up she stops. Our eyes meet. This lady is a hot ticket. I can't imagine her in a sulky.

"Are you Judy Campbell?"

When she stands up her eyes are in line with mine. She's a six-footer at least. Quite a handful, I'm sure.

"Who wants to know?" The eyes do the talking.

With my cover blown by the hoods, it is conceivable that these horsemen know who I am and why I'm here. There is no use bullshitting this gal. She looks as if she's been around.

"Sal Domino, from the NGPA, Can we talk somewhere in private?" She didn't flinch.

"You boys got real problems with these assholes. The bums have been trying to get drivers to throw races for a month. Where have you been? The management at this track, and these incompetent judges don't have a clue about any- thing. Their head is in the sand most of the time. You're cute. What did you say your name is again?" She says it with a smile.

"Just call me Sal, sweetheart. Now where can we talk?"

I follow her to the tack room. I allow her to go in first. There are several pictures of a horse on the walls scattered between bales of straw and hay, feed, and harnesses. All the pictures look to be of the same horse. I wait.

"Want a coke?" She asks.

"Sure,"

"Did you find out who killed Cotton?" Nothing like get- ting right to the point. You don't cross this lady.

 "Not yet, but I'm working on it. Where did you go the

night the murders were committed?" I already knew the answer.

"Come on copper, you already know that, don't jerk me around." I guess she's not such a lady after all.

"Okay, Judy. I know a lot. Tell me about the guy who drove your horse the other night when you were not here."

"His name is Bret Jacobs. Bret is a professional driver. He doesn't train or own horses, just drives them. He drives hard and wins a lot of races. He's the leading driver at this track. People try and buy him all the time, but he shrugs them off. He makes a better than average living doing what he's doing. I trust him with all my horses. He's a real pro. He phoned me after the race the other night, furious. He said they really "did a number on him." The crooks that were in on the race boxed him in along the rail and wouldn't let him out. He didn't wait to see the payoffs. The shit was going to hit the fan, so he booked. When he called me he was already in a diner south of town. He hasn't been back since. The judges and management want to see him pronto. I know he is innocent, but the powers to be will do what they have to do. What's your angle, Domino?" She remembers after all.

"I'm not too concerned with Jacobs. I'm interested in the guys who boxed him in. It would seem they are the culprits. I know they are only following orders and getting a piece of the action, but who is giving the orders. Do you know anything about the horse that won the race? Seems like he couldn't get out of his own way."

She doesn't hesitate.

"Jumpin' Jimmy is a nag. He hasn't won a race in six months. He's lame and has no heart. He should be a plow horse. The race department keeps entering him because he fills races. He shouldn't be racing anymore," she shouts, rather loudly.

"Are you sure it is the same horse?"

Her head tilts. A confused look crosses her face.

"I suppose it is. Gee, I didn't think about that! The state judges identify each horse by looking at the tattoo under their upper lip. I guess they can read. Why do you ask?" She stares, her eyes even with mine.

"Oh, just curious, that's all. Maybe they made a mistake and read one of the numbers wrong." I try to get her brain to move.

"They should be able to read the numbers, wouldn't you think?"

"I guess you're right."

I didn't want anyone else to hear this conversation, so I changed the subject. I point to the pictures on the walls.

"Nice horse. Is he yours?"

"That's Juniper Jane. She was the champion filly pacer three years ago. I owned her with a friend of mine. We got lucky. She is well bred, but had some physical problems so we sent her to a hotshot trainer in New York. He fixed her and turned her into a real killer. We made a bunch of money off her, and then sold her to some farm that wanted her as a broodmare. That Lexus is part of the reward. You don't think I make money at this track, do you?" She looks at me incredulously.

" I didn't think so." I say that trying to bait her. She didn't bite. "Why do you think Cotton was killed?"

"I think Cotton was in the wrong place at the wrong time. The only idea I have is that he may have overheard something and wanted to trade that info for some cash. He did drink a lot. He was a nice man. I did not have to worry about my horses when I traveled. He took good care of them, entered them to race, and worked well with Bret. I'm going to miss him," she moans.

I think a lot of people will miss Cotton. I wonder what Cotton really knew? Whatever it was cost him life. I thanked her and walked back to the guard shack.

Bill is finishing up some paper work when I appear at the

door.

"How did it go with the Campbell bitch?" I detect some animosity there. I need to know why Bill feels that way towards her.

"She tried to get cute with me, but I finally got some info from her. What's up with her Bill?"

"She's always feeding us a line of shit about taking her horses out of here and racing them somewhere else. Lying little bitch. She only stays here because there is no stall rent and she uses all the facilities. She races very few horses here and she's always on the road trying to win bigger purses. That's not fair Sal," he explains. Sounds like an internal problem to me-not my affair. I ask him if Cotton's belongings are still here. He nods and tells me to go and take a look.

This time I drove to the Groom's building. I've had enough walking today, can't spoil my image. I back in, can't take any chances in this place. As I am entering I spot Horseshoe jawing with a couple of guys, real dirtbag looking fellows. I wait until the conversation breaks up, and then slide down the hall to Cotton's room. I do not want to be spotted. I need to finish the job I started before Horseshoe interrupted me the other day. The door is ajar. I step aside and gently push open the door as I keep an eye on the hallway. The place is a damn mess. These rooms are really small, probably eight by eight. Cotton didn't have much but what he had is strewn everywhere. A mattress is turned upside down and gutted. A little hotplate is disassembled and scattered in all corners. An old piece of luggage is broken apart. Someone was looking for something. I hope they didn't find it, because I wanted to find it. I survey the mess and decide to leave the remains alone. There is no use sorting through this junk. Nothing I see looks promising to me, except the ceiling. It appears that some of the ceiling tiles have been changed or altered. There is a beat up chair in the corner. I grab it and pray it will hold my rock-hard two hundred pounds. I remove the first tile, nada. The second tile reveals nothing also. The third is a little discolored; I reach up and try to remove it. It's heavy, so I have to push it to one side. I am successful. I don't have a flashlight so I take a chance and reach in there. My hand touches a paper bag so I grab it. I replace the tile, put the bag on the floor, and give the chair a new home in another corner. Just in case, I walk to the door and check right and left, nothing there. I peek in the bag, rolled up money. I reach in and take a few bucks out to examine, c-notes, all bundled up, a whole bunch of them. Cotton knew something all right, now it's up to me to find out what it was.

When I found Olmstead's cash I left it, but not this bunch of green. The people who were looking, and didn't find it, probably won't be back. Where, how, and from whom did Cotton get all that cash? I stuff the dough under the front seat, and decide to give my brain a rest.

It is almost lunch, and I want to go to the track kitchen. I didn't know what to expect. I've only been here for a couple of days but track gossipers will have me pegged. I won't get any info out of any of these people, unless I strong-arm one of them. A lot of these transients carry a lot of baggage. If I have to, I'll dig up some dirt to help solve the case. You can usually find out anything about anyone in these environments, but they'll clam up when they figure out who I am. I walk the short distance to the track kitchen, open the door and ease in. I want to mingle and not be noticed, but it didn't work out that way.

Someone yells, "Hey copper, you're late, they already made the score!" The place broke out in an uproar. I guess they have me.

"Shut up Rabbit, or I will throw your ass out of here, for good. I'm tired of your act anyway. Do you understand?" I hear a voice behind me, it's Bill.

The dirtbag nods, and the place grows silent again.

"Didn't mean to interfere Sal, but the word is out that you

will be snooping around. You know that these guys won't give you anything but a hard time. I just tagged along when I saw you walk up."

I thank him and we adjourn to a corner seat. I leave him to grab some grub. One thing a track kitchen has is decent affordable food. You can fill your belly to last the entire day. I pay three bucks for meatloaf, mashed potatoes and a veggie and coke, not bad. I walk back to the table. I make sure I glance at the asshole that made the comment. He caught my eye and quickly turned away, cowardly bastard. I fill Bill in on the trip to Cotton's room, including discovering the cash. I didn't tell him I took it. We make small talk between bites of food. After my report we leave quickly; I didn't need any more abuse. I leave Bill at the guard shack and make the drive to the general offices. I need to talk to Bill's boss.

CHAPTER FIVE

The front of the building is neat enough, just in need of some TLC. I enter through two huge glass double doors and follow the signs that say "office." I open a green-colored door and look around. The office is tastefully decorated. I approach the desk and introduce myself, giving the receptionist one of my fancy cards that I never use. She takes the card and says the obligatory "wait a minute please." I settle in a comfortable chair to read a book on breeding of horses, how fun. The young lady comes back in a few minutes and asks me to follow her to a large office down the hall from the waiting area. I enter and am greeted by slick-looking gentlemen named Gil Holden, the General Manager. We cordially shake hands-the fencing is about to begin.

When I go to a track to work on a case I have the ability to get cooperation from all parties, the State, management, and horsemen. It is not easy because none of these parties want to share any information. The State employees are afraid of losing their jobs, the management is afraid what the event will do to their bottom-line, and the horsemen don't want to get kicked out of the track for not cooperating. I have developed several strategies to bring these parties together, sometimes it works and sometimes it doesn't, let's see what this case brings.

"It is nice of the NGPA to arrive so promptly and help to solve this case," says Holden. Yeah, right, a phony a statement as there is.

I thank him and wait for the next bullshit statement.

"Sal, our offices and employees will be at your service when and if you need anything," as the bullshit continues. "We try to police our races as best we can, but sometimes these crooks will pull one off, and it is demoralizing. The public trust is on thin ice as it is, and this event will not help the cause," he analyzes. The slick look is erased from his face. He continues. "I suppose the murders will bring in many more police agencies and I have to resign myself to the fact that I will have to answer to the various parties. Isn't that right Mr. Domino?" I can't help him there.

"You are correct, Mr. Holden, however, my agency is the only one I'm concerned about at the moment. I'm here today to learn about this track and its surroundings, and you. I will have a detailed list of questions for you later. You probably already know that Bill Beane and I have spoken a few times. He has given me several details I need to check out. Is there anything you want to tell me about before I start a full-scale investigation?" I try to read him. No go.

"No, Mr. Domino. I just want you to know that you will have my full support. My owners are throwing a fit. We are losing money at Wildwood, and they keep asking me to sell the property so that they can build a large condo development. I keep hedging because I believe that business will pick up, although this latest fiasco sets me back a tad. I am depressed about it." He finally finishes. The slick look is only a memory now. This is a troubled man. I don't envy him. I thank him and leave him with his worries. I nod at the cute little number who let me in, proceed out the door and jump in the Chevy. This will be a tough case. I have a fixed race, monies made have not yet been totaled, two murders, and some stashed cash.

It is almost time for Mary to call. I hope she found a phone she can use and not get recognized. I drive past the guard gate. As another ex-cop makes eye contact I slip onto the highway and cruise to the inn.

The drive did not take long. I smoke a cig and think about Gretchen. I wonder if she will take custody of Paul's two boys. Can they make a living? Too many questions that are none of my concern, well ....maybe....., nah forget about it

Domino, not a chance. What would a nice, educated lady want with a chain-smoking, beer-drinking fool like you? The inn appears and I turn into the lot and back in front of my room. The tape is still on the door, great, two times in a row. I turn the key, open the door and make a beeline for a brewski. Some of my colleagues think I drink too much. They are always busting my balls about it. They don't give a shit about me anyway, but they all wish I'd quit and do something else. It seems as though I embarrass them with some of my shenanigans. Tough shit, they just don't have the balls to do what they want to do. They all worry about protocol. All I know is that I've yet to lose a case, but they can stick to their protocol. In my haste to run in and grab a cold one, I didn't notice an envelope by the door. Someone must have slipped it under the door in my absence. At least they didn't break in. I walk towards the door to pick up the envelope. As I bend down, I notice that faint odor again. It smells like a cheap perfume. Maybe the smell was left over from yesterday, or maybe not. I forget about it. There is a note in a plain white envelope. I carefully read the note while holding it with the tips of my fingers. I may need to dust it sometime. The note is from Gretchen. She needs to see me ASAP. She left a number to call. I guess I don't need to worry about those prints. I shoved the note in my pocket next to the thirty-eight. The cell phone rings, right on time. I walk outside and leave the door open.

"Go ahead Mary"

"Sal, it is good to hear your voice. Are you okay?" My heart pumps. Gretchen or Mary, tough choice.

"I'm fine. No one beat me up today. Do you have any news?"

"Yes I do. It seems the agency has reported to me that there have been two more stings, one at a track in Ohio, and one in New Jersey. I'll have details in the morning."

"Good, I'm interested in them. Do they have the same MO, or not? Check it out and call me tomorrow at the same time.

Be careful Mary, remember, I suspect a leak somewhere. Only trust Jack."

"Okay, I'll dig it up. Be careful, I miss you, bye." She hangs up.

How about that, she misses me! Am I turning the corner, or what!

I walk back in the room and celebrate with another cold one and a cig. Two more stings, but no murders. These guys must be getting soft. I finish my third brewski and develop a buzz. I thought the meatloaf would absorb more than that. I change my shirt and put some cologne on. It's the same stuff I used in high school. What can I say, I like the smell. Gretchen must be disturbed about something, or she wouldn't drive down here just to leave a message. She could've told Bill. Maybe she wants to see me. Yeah, right. I dial the number. A young man with a deep voice answers. I ask to speak to Gretchen. Maybe she lives with someone. That's a depressing thought.

"Hello, this is Gretchen. Who's this please?"

She sounds great on the phone.

"It's me, Sal Domino, what do you want to talk to me about? "

"Oh, hello Sal, just a minute." I hear her tell someone named Paul to feed the dog. "I don't want the boys to hear this conversation," she rationalizes.

At least she doesn't live with anyone.

"The race department has moved me. As I was cleaning the tack room and getting ready to move to a different barn, I noticed an old set of boots that were tucked behind a bale of hay. I was going to throw them away, when I noticed some money in one of them. I took it all out, and there was several thousands dollars. Thoughts rushed through my head. Could Paul be hooked up with these thieves? I put the money in a feed bag and threw it in the back of the truck. What should I do? I need advice and help Sal. You are the only person I know who can help me, please!"

"Settle down Gretchen. Where can we meet?"

She gave me directions to her house. She would tell the boys to go to their friend's house. She lives nearby and probably slipped the note under the door on her way home. How did she know where I was staying? Bill probably told her. This is real cute. I got a bag of loot stashed under my seat in the Chevy, and she has a bag of cash in the back of a pick-up. I need to find some answers, and fast. Meanwhile, I'll be alone with her in her house.

I feel like a stupid teen-ager. The drive only takes ten minutes, but I find some landmarks so that I won't get lost on the way out. I have to remember this is a case, and this gal's brother is murdered. These scoundrels have made life miserable for these people, and I intend to put all my energy into solving the crime, that is until she looks at me. Nuts, again. The house is located on the right side of a cul-de-sac. The property looks very neat; the kids must mow and trim the yard. I make a U-turn in the cul-de-sac and park on the way out. Still can't take any chances. I bring the thirty-eight and my cigs with me in hopes she'll allow me to smoke. I ring the doorbell. The night-light comes on and the door opens. She stands in front of me with a robe on and her hair wet. Shit, my ass is in trouble. She excuses her appearance and lets me in. I notice the ashtrays in the house. She sees me looking at them and says to light up if I want to. At least I won't shake when I talk to her. She went into the bedroom to change. I light up and survey the room. Old furniture, but in decent condition. Horse pictures all over the place. There are two pictures of the boys in football uniforms; apparently they are close in age.

I'm gonna get these assholes and hang them by their balls. Watch me! She enters the room from the bedroom, her hair still a little damp. She has on jeans and a shirt. She looks good. I wait for her to say something.

"Thanks for coming, Sal. I didn't know where to turn. The

money has gotten me scared. I'm praying that Paul came into that money legally. I refuse to believe he had anything to do with the race," she says stubbornly.

"Tell me exactly what you did when you moved all the equipment today, don't leave out anything, including when and where you found the money," I say to her. She tells the story. It jives with the way I left the tack room. She describes the boots in the exact position as I saw them. She describes the money wedged in the boot, just as I left it.

"Gretchen, get the feed bag with the money in it and bring it into the house." She obeys. There has to be a clue here somewhere. I turn the bag over and empty it. There are seven bundles. We carefully unwrap them and stack the cash in rows. As Gretchen unfolds the fifth bundle, a note drops out. It reads.

"If you tell anyone what you know, your boys will die. This is the one and only payment you will receive from us.

We look at each other in amazement. Gretchen breaks down and starts sobbing. She is having a very difficult time dealing with what is happening. The death of her brother and the truth behind it is unsettling. I hug her. I didn't know what else to do. Her scent arouses me. This is no time to take advantage of a woman so I behave. I wait until she stops crying, and then offer something to drink, even though I didn't know where anything was. She wants a coke from the fridge so I go and get it. I ask her if she is well enough to continue talking, she said "okay" and continues.

"Did Paul behave strangely these past two weeks?"

"Not that I can recall. I have been on the road, shipping horses to race elsewhere because we couldn't get races here at Wildwood, nothing unusual. Wait a minute. The truck! Yes, the truck, now I remember," she blurts out. "He bought the boys a run-around pick-up, so they can go back and forth to school. They were told to share it and they're doing a pretty good job at that. I wondered where he got the money to buy it.

I asked him, and he said he got lucky and won at a card game. The problem is, I don't remember Paul ever playing cards, at least not when the stakes are that high," she explains.

We know where the money came from. I tell her to hide the money we found until we figure out what to do with it.

She seems to be feeling better now. We make some small talk and I leave. She takes my hand and thanks me. I bend over and peck her on the cheek. That is enough emotion for me and I head to my Chevy. I wave and take off.

While driving back I get some insights and really start thinking about everything I have discovered. My hunch may be right. Tomorrow morning I'll test the theory.

Before I know it I am back at the inn so I park in front of my room as usual. I have that feeling that something may not be right. I lock the Chevy; the cash is still under the seat. I get to the room and notice that the tape is off the door. The thirty-eight is in my hand as I put the key in the lock. The door is open. I step sideways and push the door all the way open. I reach for the light switch but another hand beats me to it. A different hand grabs me by the shirt and yanks me into the room. I am slammed to the floor, my side bursting with pain. Another arm gets me in a headlock. Someone else puts a blindfold around my eyes and throws me in a chair. My hands are being tied. I try to move but the grips on me are too strong. Still, nothing has been said. At best I count three sets of hands on me.

"You can't read too good, can you Domino?" says the hood. "That note didn't mean anything to you, did it asshole. Maybe we should break a few limbs, so you know we aren't screwin' around. Now listen to me you prick, I'm not gonna write anymore notes, I'm gonna tell you right here. Don't tangle with us, or our business, 'cause your ass will be shipped back to the City in five pieces, one for each borough. Do you understand?" I nod. I'm no dummy. My sides are killing me. Oh, if I only had a brew I'd show them. Just for good measure, someone clubs me across the face. I taste my blood. It tastes like beer. They untie my hands and I drop to the floor. In a matter of seconds, the room is silent. I don't hear footsteps, voices or cars, they just vanish. I drag myself to the bed and work the blindfold off my head. I feel as if I had just finished ten rounds in the ring. My body and ego are battered and bruised. I feel the blood run down the side of my mouth. I am strong enough to pull myself to the bathroom and dump some cold water on my face. I look like shit. A brew will help make the pain go away. After five beers the pain is still there.

So now what do I do? I'm not ready to die yet. The seventh brew puts me to sleep. I didn't even bother to turn the light off or take off my clothes.

CHAPTER SIX

I wake up with my head and body throbbing. The lights are still on, even though it's daylight outside. I try to get up, but the pain is excruciating. I lie there a minute and try again, this time I make it. The place is trashed. The thirty-eight is sitting by the dresser, and my phone is by the closet door. I retrieve both, being careful not to rise too quickly. I strip off my clothes and stumble to the bathroom. My insides feeling like a luau fire and my side feels like there may be a cracked rib or two. I sit in the shower until I exhaust all the hot water. Frankly, the cold water feels better. I must have sat in that tub with the water running on me for thirty minutes. I carefully get out of the tub. I won't be running the hundred-yard dash any time soon, but I am feeling better.

A look out the window reveals the wise guys weren't finished with me yet. The Chevy has four flat tires but the doors are still locked. I grab the cell phone and call the track. I ask for security. After three rings someone answered. I asked for Bill Beane. After about two minutes, Bill answers. I fill him in. He said he would be at the inn in twenty minutes. My brains are jumbled again. This is the second time these hoods have messed me up.

I hear Bill drive up. He looks at the Chevy and shakes his head. I am waiting for him at the door.

"Jesus, Sal. They did a number on you. I know a Doc who'll look at you and keep it off the records. You want me to give him a call?" I nod. I drape a shirt over my body and slowly make my way to Bill's beater. The door creaks open and I sit my sorry ass in the front seat. Bill cranks up the beater, surprised it even starts. We scoot off. The Doc isn't far. He

is retired and does favors for people from time to time. Bill
uses him when he has someone he wants to be tested for
drugs, or is high on drugs. Bill doesn't turn them into the
State. If they cross him, they're finished. A lot of people in the
backstretch owe Bill Beane lots of favors. We stop in front of
a very distinguished looking two-story Tudor. Bill helps me
up the steps; rings the bell, and the door opens quickly. A tall
gray-haired gentleman helps me to a small treatment room.

"What do we have here Bill? Can you sit up son?" he asks.
I nod. He pokes and prods and I scream and yell. After the
exam he tells me that I have two cracked ribs and a mild concussion. He wraps the ribs and advises rest, the only cure. I
am to stay bedridden for at least a week. I didn't argue, but as
Bill and I look at each other we know that would be impossible. I thank him and walk out of his office on my own.

Before we drive back to the inn Bill calls a garage to
arrange for the tires to be replaced. At least I will get new rub-
ber in the deal. He asks me if I am hungry and I shake my
head no. When we arrive at the inn the garage people are
already fixing the tires. We go into the room and wait for
them to finish. I fill him in on the attack. I tell him I didn't
recognize any of the voices. I also tell him about Gretchen and
the money and about Cotton's money. I need his help so I lay
it on the line.

We agree that these boys are playing too rough for me.
The only reason I'm alive is that I'm a federal agent. You don't
go around casually knocking feds off. We also agree that I
should move from the inn before I lose all of my ribs. Bill
suggests his place. He has an apartment in the back of his
property he keeps for his kids when they come home from
college. Ellie is happy to have me stay. I can't argue, considering the condition I'm in. We also agree not to tell anyone, and
that includes Mary and Jack from the agency. We decide to
leave room 21 like it is, to make people believe that I left in a
hurry. I leave all the clothes and toiletries. I am still bothered

by that perfume smell in the room.

I thank the garage men and tell them I'd be by later this week and settle up. I follow Bill to his house. We arrive and I drive the Chevy around back by the room so it can't be seen from the road. I climb out of the Chevy, very gingerly. Ellie is waiting for us and gives me a great big hug.

"Easy now Ellie", the ribs hurt! It's good to see her again. Behind every successful man is a strong woman, I know it's a cliché, but it's true. Bill is a very lucky man. Ellie fixes some coffee and I relax in a nice large bed. She tells me that she'll have clothes and toiletries for me in the morning. I drift off to sleep, and I finally feel safe. Mary's evening call will go unanswered. I'll explain to her tomorrow, if I get up.

The night goes quickly. I open my eyes to sunlight at around 9:00 a.m. I never sleep until nine, except when I'm aching from being beat up. I try to get up, but my body is not cooperating. Ellie must have seen me struggling through the window and she appears, holding a cup of coffee. I am scantily clad, but I figure she's seen skin before. I thank her for the great tasting java and go back to struggling with my balance. I try to gather my thoughts about the events that occurred yesterday. I want to forget about yesterday, but it's difficult, considering the constant pain that reverberates throughout my body. Gretchen races through my mind. She doesn't know how close she came to trouble last night. These assholes know my every move, and no doubt they know I was with her last night. What they don't know, I hope, is that we have the money.

Ellie appears with another cup of coffee. She has to have ESP. Clothes and toiletries are brought and tossed on the bed. I thank her again, still standing in my underwear. The apartment comes equipped with a hot shower. I jump in and I am careful around the area where I am slugged. I towel off and try the clothes on; a nice fit, but a little snug. Bill is a couple of inches shorter and a dozen or so pounds lighter than I am. The Nikes match the outfit. I stroll out the door, not bothering to lock it. I walk to the main house where Ellie is fixing a brunch. My stomach growls as I smell the vittles. We eat in silence. I sit on the porch, wrapped like a damn mummy, smoking a cig when Bill drives up in the beater.

"You look a hell of a lot better than you did last night," he says.

" I feel better, thanks to some home remedy from Ellie. She's a peach," I note. " Everything is first class."

"What are you going do now?" A legitimate question from Bill.

"Before the beating last night I started thinking. Bill, suppose that Jumpin' Jimmy isn't really Jumpin' Jimmy. Suppose the punks devised a plan to switch horses, or do something else. I'm not sure what, but something that would fool the public and the other horsemen in the race. Can that be done?" I ask, seriously.

He has a curious look on his face. He is deep in thought.

"Sal, before every race the paddock judge will turn the top lip of all the horses in a race, and check a tattoo. That tattoo is put there at a young age to certify that this horse is the horse that is registered. I have never heard of any switching or any chicanery in that respect. That doesn't mean that these guys couldn't have devised a plan that would work in this situation. A lot of people would have to be in on the scam," he describes.

I try to get what he's saying. He's right, a lot of people would have to be involved. I'm still in thought as Bill leaves to get back to the track to set up for racing tonight. Bill's very particular when it comes to the shipping of horses in and out for races. He has tight control and strict procedures, his guards know the routine. Some of these trainers will lie through their teeth.

I walk back to the apartment, pop a few pills, and take a snooze. I don't miss the brew yet, but the urge is coming back. I sleep until 5:00 p.m. When I get up this time I feel a bit more coordinated. Ellie says I can smoke, so I light up. Mary will call soon, so I have to be ready to explain why I didn't answer the call last night. I turn the phone on and wait. Bill comes up the driveway and bypasses the house and comes directly to the apartment.

"You look better. How are the ribs?" I nod, but don't talk.

"Gretchen stopped by the guard shack and asked for you. I told her there has been a change of plans. I invited her out to the house this evening. My lieutenant is covering me tonight so the three of us can have talk tonight. I hope you don't mind that I asked her to come by. Sal, we can trust her, I know that for a fact." I nod again, but don't talk. "I have been thinking over what you said about the tattoos. This is a good question for Gretchen to answer. If there is a trick, she can give us some insight into it. Get some more rest, because it will be a late night," he commands. I nod for the third time, then lie on the bed and wait for Mary to call.

Mary is prompt, as usual. The phone rings once, I answer.

"Go ahead. Have you got some news?"

"Hi Babe, (I'm a babe now). Boy, I got some goods for you. The two races I told you about have the same MO. A long shot wins the race, while the favorites run up the track or get boxed in and the winning combinations go through the roof. It is surmised that several million have been won, counting the race at Wildwood. That means these crooks have made a score at three tracks, and I'm sure they are not going to stop." she explains. "How's it going up there? Why didn't you answer the phone last night? I am worried. Are you doing okay?" she persists.

"I'm fine," lying through my teeth. There is no reason why she needs to know what happened. I can't trust my agency if there is a leak, so I won't use her. I will have to pacify her everyday. She can still furnish some details when needed, but I will not jeopardize her life.

" Mary, call the wagering departments of the two tracks

and see if they can trace who has cashed any winning tickets at the track. Ask to talk to the Wagering Facilitator and have each track furnish us with a printout of the winning combinations, have them overnight mail them to you. I doubt any tickets are being cashed on track. They are being cashed off track at any number of locations all over the country. If we start tracking down all the cashed tickets we'll be on this case for a year. Got it?"

"Okay. I'll get right on it. You sound different. Are you sure you're okay?" she persists.

"I'm fine. Call me tomorrow at the same time." dodging the question rather deftly. I also didn't tell her I moved. She'll ask too many questions and I will have to give answers I don't want to give.

I lit a cig and lay down for a few minutes. Bill did not give me a time for the party, but it must be approaching. Just as I say that, I hear a vehicle drive up. It stops in front of the house. I hear the door creak open, and am reminded what Gretchen's truck door sounds like. I wash my face again, carefully eluding the sore spot, and brush my hair. I still look like shit. I walk the short distance to the main house. I hear murmuring in the kitchen. I stop for a moment to compose myself, then enter where they are yakking. Gretchen turns and looks at me. She gasps, while putting her hand over her mouth. I guess I must be scary looking.

"Sal, what happened?" she shouts. Bill and Ellie wait for me to handle the situation. Gretchen races to me and gives me a big hug. I grimace in pain, but didn't let on that she grabbed my broken ribs.

"I'll explain later. Bill, can we have some drinks?" The burning won't go away. After getting requests, Ellie brings a tray full of libations. We all have a drink, and make small talk. Ellie says that dinner will be served in thirty minutes. The small talk becomes livelier, when Gretchen and Bill start mocking my beloved Jets and the Tuna. I stand my ground.

We all laugh, even I do, as I clutch my ribs. Dinner is marvelous. Ellie bakes some snapper with boiled potatoes and a salad. I need the food for strength. The food has a tough time fitting in my stomach because I'm wrapped like a mummy. I did the best I could, Ellie understands.

Bill and I start asking Gretchen some difficult questions.

"Gretchen, is it possible that a horse, or horses, can be switched in a race? Can the registration of a horse get misplaced? Can a tattoo be altered to read differently? Would you shed some light on the subject? The thought raced through my mind last evening when we were messing around with that damn money."

I wait for a response. It is quite obvious that the questions took her by surprise. She is very silent then speaks, carefully.

"The chances of any of that happening are very slim Sal. I haven't heard of a case where there has been a discrepancy with respect to the registration, or entry of a horse. When a horse is a yearling, his lip is turned upwards and numbers are tattooed on the lip. These are distinguishing features that will be with a horse until it dies. The numbers are large enough to read, and for the most part, clearly legible. Because horses race in so many states, each state has its own particular way of handling these details. It is common practice that when a horse travels his registration papers follow him. The tattoo reaffirms that this is the horse on that registration. It is very difficult to change anything I have mentioned. What are you driving at?" she asks, after the explanation.

"Paul stumbled across something he wasn't supposed to find out about. Perhaps he overheard people talking, or actually witnessed an illegal act, we'll never know. The note we discovered last night indicates to me he knew of a fix, and how it was going to be arranged. I think that when he entered that race he knew what was going down. Instead of tipping his hand by scratching his horse, he intentionally broke stride on the first turn. Someone was going to do a number on him, and instead of risking bodily harm, he removes himself from the action. The wise guys have one less person to block in that race. Paul did it himself. He figures he can explain to the judges why the horse broke stride. After the race, he is approached in the barn area and killed. Did Paul want to extort more money from the fixers? We'll never know the answer to that or many other questions; we can only surmise." I finished and watched her expression very closely. She is trying to determine if I am implicating Paul, or making an excuse for him. I hope it is the latter. She composes herself and answers.

"Are you saying that Paul knew about a fixed race and didn't tell anyone?" she yells. "Is that what you are saying Sal? Is it?"

"No, Gretchen, that is not what I'm saying. I'm saying that what he discovered cost him his life. He may have uncovered something by just observing it. However, I can't explain the money. I wish I had an answer for that. Let me try and pick your brain a little more. If this is too hard for you, let us know and we will stop anytime, (she stares straight ahead). Did Paul have a safe at home or a safety deposit box where that he keeps important stuff?"

The look is blank as she thinks hard. Her face brightens a little and she answers.

"Yes, I may know of a place. It certainly isn't that smelly boot we found, but Paul used to stash some papers away in a strongbox at our farm. I don't know where it may be or if anything's in it."

"That's super Gretchen!" I say happily.

"I want you to draw a map of the farm so that Bill can go and check it out. Make it as detailed as you can. I want to know where every fence post, stall, feed room etc. is located. Bill will go and snoop around. Please alert the boys that he will be coming there. Okay?" She nods.

"Ellie, why don't we watch a movie together in the rack,

and let these younguns' get to know each other better." Ellie smiles and they leave.

Shit, now what do I do? I'm gonna get Bill for this, the old rascal planned this whole deal. He's a grumpy ole man, but I love it. Here goes!

"Ellie fixed up a nice apartment for me in the back. Maybe we can bring a few drinks back there and chew this over a bit more." I read her look, but she said it anyway.

"I'll go back with you Sal, but I don't want to talk anymore," she fetches the drinks to bring back with us. My ass is in trouble, I just hope that I can handle it.

I helped her with the tray. She likes scotch and soda, and of course, I have the brewskis. I bring more than the usual amount in case I get scared. The nightlight is on as we make our way to the apartment. Not a word is spoken. I open and hold the door for her as she brings the booze in. She put the tray down on a table then stands up to look me square in the eye. I froze. Hell, I'm supposed to solve a case, not get involved. I took her hand and gently drew her close to me. We kiss briefly, sort of like a get to know you kiss. The fireworks will start later, I hope. I lit up. She didn't protest. She broke the ice.

"I haven't been with a man in a long time, but I feel safe with you. I don't want to interfere with your solving this case. Do you like me Sal?"

Now, how do I handle that!

"You have been a great help to me and Bill. You answered some tough questions tonight, I know that wasn't easy for you. Gretchen, I promise you, I'll find these guys and string 'em up. You are an extraordinary woman and now you will have to run a farm, manage a racing stable and raise two teen-age boys. That, in and of it self is remarkable. I hope I can ease your burden by solving this case." How about that, Domino is emotional.

She put her arms around me. It is then that she feels the

mummy.

"Does that hurt?" she asks. I nod. "Well allow me to make you feel a whole lot better." I forget about the brews, cigs, Mary, the case and everything else in the world. We succumb to our urges and enjoy the evening together.

CHAPTER SEVEN

I am awakened by the sound of running water and the scent of a woman. I haven't smelled that aroma since my wife left me several years ago. I don't talk about her much. She was right in deciding that she wanted a husband who was home cuddling her, well. I sure wasn't that guy. Our marriage only lasted a few short years. My work kept me on the go all the time. She didn't accept that way of life and I couldn't blame her. I heard she got remarried --a pharmacist in Gary, Indiana. I miss the smell, especially when it is coming from a lady like Gretchen. I can smell my soap and shampoo as she cleanses the sex off her body. I wonder if I was any good? We hardly spoke, just two lonely people connecting for a memorable experience.

She steps out of the shower with a towel wrapped around her. Her natural beauty is a sight to behold. I really can't get involved with anyone, I just can't. I would not want any woman to be in danger because of the work that I do. I have been beaten up several times, shot at, threatened with bombs attached to my car and other personal attacks. Why would a woman want to be subjected to a life like that? After seventeen years in this racket I have made some enemies. I don't want a lady putting up with that crap, I'll go it alone.

She murmurs, "I've got to get to the stable. That work is not going to get done by it self. The boys will be there after school, but everything will be done by then. They can feed the horses for the night, and freshen up the stalls. That will keep them busy for awhile." She looks casually at me, as if we are long lost buddies. I hope she doesn't have any expectations. "What are your plans?"

"Do you know anything about the trainer-driver of Jumpin' Jimmy?" I ask in the same casual manner. "It is about time I visit the stable to see if my suspicions may be correct." She drops her towel to get dressed. As she snaps her bra, she speaks.

"Yes, I do. His name is Butch Green. He has been in lots of trouble over the years and has been tossed out of a few tracks. Why they allow him to race here is beyond me. He's always been on the edge and the only reason he is racing here is his stable. He has lots of horses to race and he fills races for the race department when they need help. He has over thirty horses, a large staff, and deep pockets."

"Thanks for the info," We both kind of look at each other rather awkwardly for a second. "I'll be staying here for the duration of my visit. No one, I mean no one, is to know where I'm staying. Is that clear Gretchen?" The look says it all.

"Of course I do Sal. I would not jeopardize you, or your health for all the fixed races in this country. Do you understand that?" I sure do. We smile at each other. She walks to the bed and pecks me on the cheek, then she is gone.

It seems easier to get up this morning. Must have been the sex and loving I received the night before. I have chills just thinking about it. I smoke a cigarette while I'm trying to shave. I have to navigate the area that is sore--not as bad today.

While in the shower I'm thinking about a plan. The visit to Butch Green's stable will be fairly difficult, but I need to look at Jumpin' Jimmy. Maybe Bill can help me get to see him.

I dress quickly and I open the door and Ellie is standing there with the coffee. She smiles. I guess she figured out what went on last night. I thank her, gulp the coffee and scoot. The Doc who treated me will have to realize that I can't be bedridden for a week. I'll play the mummy, but I've got to hit the road. The Chevy cranks and we are off. The thirty-eight is pissed because he got roughed up a bit too, but he feels better under my shoulder where he belongs. I drive to the track.

I nod to the guard. He allows me to pass without suspicion. Bill's beater is parked at the guard shack. I pull in and he greets me as I open the door.

"Well looky here! The stud," he shouts at me. I blush.

"Com'on, knock it off. You set me up, you old goat."

"Tell me you didn't like it, then I'll apologize." I smile.

"Let's get to business. Where do I find Butch Green's stable? It's time to shake him up a bit. Do you have any idea how I can take a look at the area without being obvious?" Bill is thinking.

"Yes, I do. Remember that big black guy that scared the shit out of you in the groom's building? Well, he's a groom for Butch, and he does his shoeing for him. Wait a second," Bill says as he goes into the office. "You can use this on Horseshoe. I busted him for drugs awhile back. I use him when I need some info. I kept his case in house and didn't turn it over to the feds and he still owes me. If he gives you a hard time, spring this on him," Bill explains. He hands me some papers. This will work out for me.

Green is located in barn X, way up on a hill, far from the training track and the main building. Seems a far walk when you have so many horses. I make a U-turn at the top of the hill and park on the downhill, pointing out. I can't take any more chances, like that's even an option any longer. The emergency brake works. The thirty-eight is ready if I need him. Getting out of the Chevy on a downhill isn't easy when you're feeling like I do. The stable is bustling. Horses are everywhere, coming and going to the training track. Stalls are being cleaned, horses are being washed and equipment cared for. There must be five grooms working feverishly. I hear a high-pitched voice giving orders on the other side of the barn. The voice appears in the form of a slightly built man in his forties. He is ranting and raving to all of his help. I hope he pays well for that abuse. I walk to where the commotion is going on.

"Butch Green?" I ask. I spot Horseshoe standing in a stall. He glares at me. I'm sure he knows who I am and that I'm not a bookie. His stares are almost as fearful as his hands. I ignore him. There is plenty of time for him. I've got to get a beat on Green to see if I can detect anything.

"I'm Green. Who wants to know?"

I flash my credentials that I don't like to use. He doesn't blink.

Horseshoe is still glaring at me.

"Mr. Domino, is it?" Good morning, how can I help the NGPA?" as smooth as a con man can say it.

"We need to talk somewhere in private, right now," trying to put my best Bogart on him. It works.

"Let's walk to the fence up there. That should be private enough and I can still keep an eye on these guys" he reasons. It appears innocent enough. So I follow him. Horseshoe's eyes follow me.

"Nice operation you have here, Green. Lots of horses, I bet you make a good living here at Wildwood," trying to bait him.

"The purses here aren't too big, so it's important to race a lot of horses to pick up checks." He cocks his head, away from the sun and continues. "Domino, I don't have to fix races to live."

"Who said anything about fixing races Butch?" I say, flatly.

"Why else would you be jawing with me. My horse won a fixed race, so I figured you guys would be around sooner or later. Right?"

"Let's just say I'm covering all the bases and talking to a lot of people. I'm going to gather as much info as I can, you know what I mean Butch?" I say sarcastically. He's smooth.

"Sure, Domino. I get the drift. Poke around all you want. You ain't gonna find anything on me."

"I plan to Butch, I'll be looking real hard around here."

He flashes me a big, wide smile, as if to say, "good luck, sucker." He leaves. As I walk down the hill, Horseshoe is still glaring at me. I swear, if people weren't around he would crush me like a grape. I'll bait the big oaf. I need to talk to him when he gets down off that hill. Bill told me where his blacksmith shop is so I'll wait for him there.

I didn't have to wait long. He came lumbering down the hill. I think I hear the ground shake. I parked the Chevy at the guard shack. I am hiding on the side of his shop, when I hear the door open. I pop around and surprise him. I push his big ass in the door. When he turns around, the thirty-eight is staring him in the face.

" Alright boss, I ain't movin'. I've felt one of those before, and I don't like 'em. You lied to me, copper. You ain't no book-ie, you a cop," he shouts angrily. "Why you playin' with ole Horseshoe?   I got nothin' for you." He tries to lower his hands. When he sees the look on my face, they go up again.

"Oh, you're going to help me Horseshoe." as I wave the papers in front of him. I didn't want to get too close.

"What you got there, copper? Wipe your ass with them papers."

"Bill Beane thought I might need these if you are going to be stubborn. It says something about some drugs. Now, Horseshoe, you don't fool with drugs, do you?" I ask, sarcastically.

"You rotten cop bastard. I ought to rip those papers right out of your hand. That gun won't fell me with one shot. You better be prepared to shoot 'em all if you want me down. Then if I land on you, what you gonna do? Can you move three hundred fifty pounds, copper? Huh. What you gonna do?" he says defiantly.

"You want to find out?" I say, just as defiantly. We stare at each other. It seems like hours. He isn't going to budge. I really am going to have to shoot this big asshole. Just when I thought it is hopeless, he smiles.

"Now, looky here, copper. Maybe we can make a deal, huh."

"I'm holding the cards, Horseshoe, I don't make deals."

"What if I give you some info that will help you. Ya know; Cotton was a friend of mine. I don't like nobody goin' round breakin' necks. Ya know what I mean copper?"

"What kind of info?"

"If I do help you, will you rip up those papers? I'm a two-time loser. If the feds find out about that drug deal, my black ass is goin' to jail. They'll rape this nigger 'till I die. I don't want that."

"I'll think about it, what do you have for me? It better be good, or your ass won't be tight anymore, I'll see to that."

"Suppose I tell you that Jumpin' Jimmy, ain't really Jumpin' -Jimmy. What do you say to that copper?"

My heart is racing. I felt there was something fishy. I don't want to show that I'm excited in front of him. I got to be cool.

"That's a tall statement, Horseshoe. What proof do you have?"

"Do we have a deal, copper, about the papers?"

" It depends on how strong the info is. What makes you so sure that Jumpin' Jimmy is a different horse?"

"I groom all these horses, and shoe them too. I know which horse is which, I know them like the back of this black hand. That horse ain't Jumpin' Jimmy. The real Jumpin' Jimmy can't race like that horse. I know what I know from inside," he says, confidently

"We didn't have this talk, do you understand?" I say, strongly.

"If I find out you are talking to anyone about anything, I'll hang your ass on general principles. You got it?" He nods. I slip out the door. I pack the thirty-eight away and walk to the guard shack. I'm hungry, but I don't dare go to the track kitchen. Bill's beater isn't there. I nod at the guard as I drive out. I need a brewski. I decide to go to a joint on the outskirts of town and clear my mind.

The Paddock Bar is a hangout for horsemen and the likes. If there is to be any business done it usually takes place in a joint like this. The lot is circular, so I am sure to park at an angle to pull out quickly, if I need to. The joint is jumpin'. Redneck music is blaring from an over-used jukebox and the noise is deafening. I hope these guys pay their bills before they drink up the profits. I keep a low profile and try to mix with the crowd. I wear my Mets baseball cap to hide me. I order a brew at the bar and start to walk through the crowd. Somebody is tugging at my shirt. It's Judy Campbell. What is she doing in a place like this? I'm fixing to find out.

"Well, copper, fancy meeting you in a place like this. Did you catch the killers yet? You will find all sorts of people willing to talk to you in here." she says sarcastically. "Can I buy you a beer?" I nod and follow her to a small booth in the rear of the bar. She puts her purse on the table in front of me, and fetches the drinks. Boy, would I like to snoop in that thing! She returns with a tray filled with glasses and a picture of brew, my kind of girl.

"Well, you didn't answer the question."

"I am on my way home from the track, and decided to stop for a cold one. Is there any law that says a cop can't have a beer?"

"Easy now, fella. I am only playing." My look says I'm not in the playing mood. She changes the subject. "How about we have some fun and try and forget all this mess. I live a short way from here. Do you want to come over and share a case of Bud with me and fool around? I think I can handle a raw-boned fella like you," she brags. The thought is repulsive to me. This is her environment. She plays the role, trying to be miss hot shot, but she's nothing but a hustling bitch, just as Bill described her. A good cop is rarely wrong. I look at my watch, then graciously decline. I get up to leave. As soon as I leave, some young stud who will take her up on her hustle takes my seat. She didn't bat an eye, a real pro. I open the door to find the Chevy. I see it and start to walk toward it but someone stops me.

"Hey, copper. I don't like your ass snooping around my barn," "keep your ass off of barn X or I'll beat your ass, " says Butch Green. I guess Butch can't hold his liquor. I hear people trying to move him on, but he persists. "Copper, I'm talking to you."

I walk up to where he is standing. His thugs are ten paces from my Chevy.

"Butch, for a little shit, you got a big mouth. I'll look any- where I want to, punk. And if I find anything, I'll cuff your skinny ass." He can't take the last remark. He breaks free from the guy who is holding him and charges me. He lunges with his right fist closed. That leaves his side open and I nail him with a good shot to the kidney. He drops like melted butter and barfs all over himself. His henchmen make a move toward me but the thirty-eight is ready. He loves the action. They freeze, then I speak.

"Get this punk ass outa here. I'll see him in the morning, if he can get up. If you boys are carrying, you better forget it. I'll bust every one of you assholes, now get outa here." The com- motion causes a group of people to gather around. Someone comes forward and speaks.

"Listen Domino, I run a clean place here. Butch likes to drink and run his mouth too much, he didn't mean no harm, honest. Isn't that right folks?" the barkeep says. I hear mur- muring as they all agree. I stare the barkeep down. I'm sure Butch tips him just so he can come in here and run his mouth. I'm sure I'm not the only guy who has popped him. I walk backward to the Chevy, keeping everyone in sight. I unlock the Chevy, climb in, and drive away. This is a hostile group at this track. My ribs are a little tender because I had to extend in order to clip the punk. A brew will take care of that.

A look at my watch indicates it is 7:00 p.m. Mary didn't

call. I reach for the phone and realize it is dead. I'll have to explain in the morning. I hope she is okay. Jack and Mary have got to be careful. I drive to Bill's house. I am surprised when I see Gretchen's truck parked in front. I'm excited, but why would she be here tonight?

I pull around back. As I open the door, she appears and speaks first.

"Bill has some news for us. We waited, hoping you would show up. I'm glad you came." Her look is genuine. I freshen up then walk to the main house where Bill is sitting at the table going over some papers. Gretchen is with Ellie preparing coffee for us. I join the group.

"Sal, we may have a clue. Gretchen drew a great map of the property. I went out there this morning while the boys were in school so that I could find my way around the property. I found my way to the barn, there are eight stalls and I checked them out. In the seventh stall the ground feels different. I snoop around with a shovel and notice that there is a false floor. I push away the bedding and find a four-foot square board with a handle on one side. I gently lift the handle. There is an assorted bunch of memorabilia about baseball and horses. At the bottom of the pile is a saddlebag. I lifted the bag to examine the contents. The left side has a wad of cash in it. Rolled up c-notes like you found in his barn. (Gretchen shudders). In the right side is this note. It reads:

If someone finds this note, that means I'm dead. There is plenty of money for Gretch and the boys to live on. Here's my story. I am working at the barn late one night, when I notice a van pull up. It's awful late for shipping, so I walk to the barn where I see the van. A horse exits. I think to myself, that's Jumpin' Jimmy. I've always liked that horse. I was going to buy him for Gretch to ride. I know how much she likes to do that. Jimmy can't race anymore; he's too sore. Boy he looks sprightly, I think to myself. When they finish unloading him, I take a peek at him. It isn't Jumpin Jimmy. He can be his twin, but it isn't Jimmy. When I drew into the race with Jimmy, I am apprehensive. I am warming up my horse before the race and I see this horse that looks like Jimmy. He's entered as Jimmy. Something is going down. I make up an excuse to scratch my horse from that race. The state vet looks at my horse. I say he is lame, and he agrees. I watch the race and Jimmy runs up the track, but its not Jimmy. I take my horse and walk back to the barn. Someone is setting up to make a big score. I hid in my barn until they came back with the horse. I can recognize Green's voice, but no one else. They leave, then I walk to Jimmy's stall. I am amazed. This horse in front of me is not Jimmy, yet he is almost identical. This is a ringer! I decide to approach Green the next day. He denies all that I say, but will not allow me to look at Jimmy. I call him an asshole and leave. The next morning, a large man wearing sunglasses approaches my barn. He gives me a bag and leaves. I don't recognize him, nor have I seen him again. How did he get in the barn area? He didn't say a word. The bag is full of money with a threatening note. I hide the money. Some of it I put in the stable at the track in a boot, and you have found the rest. We draw into the same race the following week. I am scared. Is this the race they are going to collect? I am the favorite in the race. I think about the boys and Gretch. I have heard stories about fixed races. The paddock is quiet, unusually quiet before the race. I warm up my horse. Jimmy, who is not Jimmy, is warming up also. He looks great on the track. Shit, that isn't Jimmy. I drew the eight hole in this race. When we are behind the starting gate in the sulkies, I feel Green looking at me. Now I'm really scared. The starter yells at me to get my horse up to the gate. It's too late to scratch again. I'm scared even more. The race goes off. I break alertly. I need to be away from Green and whoever he has bought in the race. I don't know who they are. I know it isn't Bret or me. Bret is a solid guy. By the time I get to the first turn, my nerves are frazzled. I jerk the reins and break my horse. She starts to run. I'm trailing the field some ten lengths when she finally hits stride again. I felt like I may have saved my life at that point. I came in dead last. The people start to boo me as I cross the finish line. Boy, if they only knew. I stayed to myself after the race. I hear the booing at the grandstand. I see a fire. I can only guess; at that point, the winning prices are way out of line. I ignore Green. I want to get away from there as fast as I can. They didn't have to 'do a number on me'. I did it myself. I feel like shit. I never cheat. I always race honestly, but this race is an exception. I'm embarrassed for all the honest horsemen who make an honest living. This race is a travesty. I hope they find the people behind it. Green is only a small potato. That was not Jumpin' Jimmy that night. It was a ringer! Find out how they did it. I love all my family. Gretch, I know the money is dirty, but use it anyway. Bye

Love, Paul.

CHAPTER EIGHT

When Bill finished, he bowed his head and said, "May God have mercy on his soul." We are all in a state of shock. The events described by Paul are frightening. And this has happened all over the country. Several millions of dollars have been scammed from the public, and people are dead because of it. Gretchen is in bad shape. Ellie takes her into the living room and tries to comfort her. It will be several hours until she is herself. I want to hold her, but Ellie glances at me and slowly shakes her head. That is the signal for me to stay out of the way. It's not everyday a person's death letter is read to a loved one. I would not know how to handle it. I need a drink.

Ellie guides Gretchen to a spare bedroom where she is given a sleeping pill. Ellie returns to the table and informs us that Gretchen will no longer be available to us. Bill and I have not spoken a word since he read the note. I have to break the ice.

"Ellie, will Gretchen be okay here tonight? I don't want her driving in her condition." Ellie nods.

"Bill, We have got to find Bret Jacobs. He is hiding somewhere, afraid to surface. I will not talk to that Campbell lady again. You are right, she is a royal bitch. Do we have any contacts that will help us find Jacobs?" Bill wakes up from his stupor.

"Let me think on it for awhile. I will go to the track in the morning and look up his file and see if he has anyone listed on his application who lives close by," I agree.

I walk outside and light up. Damn, where is that beer. Green is obviously the key, but as Paul described in his note, he is a small potato in the overall scheme. I am exhausted.

The letter took a lot out of us, especially Gretchen. I wait patiently for the beer and Ellie delivers. The look on my face tells her this will be a several beer night. I walk to the apartment and extra brewskis arrive shortly. I thank Ellie and start to consume. My brain starts to deaden after number four, and completely shuts down after number six. At least I turn the light off and remove my clothes this time.

I hear a car start and look at the clock. It's 6:00 a.m. and Bill is already off to the track. I might as well get up. The brews put me to sleep and deadened the rib pain, but I feel it this morning. I throw on some clothes and walk to the main house. I open the back door and the smell of fresh coffee greets me. As I am helping myself to the java, Gretchen walks in. She looks like hell, but I will not tell her that. She's pretty even looking like hell, ah nuts…. forget about it. I spoke.

"You aren't going to the track, are you?" I ask.

"Of course I am, the work can't get done by itself. The boys should be in school, and the work has to be completed," she says

"Do you know where I can find Bret Jacobs?"

"I do not know Bret very well. Paul used to talk about him all the time because Bret can really drive a horse. Paul wished he had his talent. Maybe Bill can find something out," she says, really not interested in Bret. I nod.

We leave in separate vehicles because I don't want anyone to see us together. Her life may be in jeopardy. I want to be sure she arrives at the barn safely, so I drive a short distance behind her. When she's okay, I'll swing to Bill's shack.

The beater is parked in front of the guard shack. Bill pops out of the office to greet me.

"I had to speak to the Presiding Judge and his flunkies this morning. They wanted to know how I was progressing with the case. I told them that I was gathering evidence. They didn't like the answer, because they are in the dark. They want me to do all the digging, then they get the credit, typical politicians. I didn't tell them shit. If they send in their boys from NYC do you have jurisdiction?" I nod. "Good, that means we will have control of the situation." I nod, again.

"Did you find out anything about Jacob's whereabouts?"

"Not yet, I have been jackin' with those idiots all morning."

"I suppose I will have to visit them, just as a matter of courtesy," I say. "I'll be with them if you need to find me," and stomp out of the office.

Because of the fixed race the judges have moved to an office by the race department. This office, in the backstretch, gives them the freedom to question any licensee of the state. They think they have power and influence over people, but they really don't. The judges usually are political appointees of the state in which they reside. Their knowledge is limited to the statutes they have to uphold, in the state where they hold office. Their knowledge of any racing or wagering activity is limited and they are not expected to know all the ins and outs, but to know and uphold the law. In this respect, they have the ability to 'hold' any person's license until that party cooperates. Sometimes it works; sometimes it doesn't. In this case, I doubt any of their influence will work. The presiding judge at Wildwood is a gruff old man who has been a state employee for over twenty-five years. He plays by the book and won't go out on a limb for anyone. He covers his ass at every corner, typical politician.

I drive to their office and don't back in. The race department is bustling, trying to fill a race card to the track's satisfaction. With the judges being so close, it cramps their style, meaning they can't pull any fast ones that may result in bending a rule to fill a race with the proper number of horses. The race department is patient with their presence. I get a glimpse of the Race Secretary, whose job it is to put the races together, and he rolls his eyes at me. Bill apparently told him who I am, because I don't know the guy.

I enter the judge's office. There are three guys standing around, not doing a damn thing. It's a scary thought, but they actually get paid big money to stand around and do nothing. The burly, gruff man raises his head and sees me enter. He glances at his flunkies and they disperse, leaving us alone. I speak.

"Judge Pete Masterson, I presume," I say, playfully. He isn't playing.

"Hello Domino, I've been expecting you. How come it took you so long to get to me. You know I run this track." The general manager would love to hear that.

"Sorry, judge, I didn't know I had to check in with you." I say, sarcastically." Can we talk here?" He nods and starts.

"I want to know what information you can give me with respect to this case. I expect you to hand over everything you've got," he demands.

I'm taken aback. The arrogance is a little too much for me. I will have to hold my temper, realizing that these guys are political and can be re-appointed in another capacity elsewhere in the bureaucracy. They all fear for their jobs. I remain cool, knowing I may need this clown myself.

"Judge, I haven't formulated any plan yet, so there is little I can give you in the way of info."

"Bullshit, Domino. You have been here for three days and you're telling me the great Domino hasn't come up with anything. That is true bullshit!" he shouts. "Now come clean!" I try to stay calm.

"Despite what you may have heard, this case is a difficult one, and will need all my experience to solve. And, furthermore, if you shout at me again, I'll have your damn job. I do, and will continue to have jurisdiction in this matter. Is that clear?" So much for their damn influence.

He stares at me, as if that political stare will rattle me. I stare right back.

"You're a wise ass, Domino, and I don't like it. You parade

around this country ignoring all the laws we are supposed to uphold, just to feed your own ego. You break more rules and laws than the people you are sent out to catch. You're nothing but a hoodlum with a badge!" I thought I told him not to yell at me. I wait for him to calm down before I go at him again.

"You're allowed to have your own opinion of me, and I don't give a shit what you think. I don't break any rules or laws, I just bend them a little and that works for me, and the agency. I am successful because I don't listen to political blowhards like you. I deal in facts, not political conjecture. I'll be in touch if I need you." Then, I march out. The race department hears the shouting. The Race Secretary, who spotted me as I came in rolled his eyes at me again, this time I wink at him.

I drive back to the guard shack and report to Bill. He roars with laughter. He always wanted to get that pompous asshole himself, I save him the trouble. He has information on where to find Jacobs. He has to talk to the Campbell lady. He detests that woman so I know it isn't easy for him. Jacob drove her horse on that night, so he picks her brains. It seems that Jacob has a sister who lives about an hour away in a little town called Cyprus. I got the directions to the town, and the name and phone number of the sister. I did not want to talk to Gretchen, and I tell Bill to make an excuse for me if he sees her. My cell phone is recharged, so I told him I would call if I find anything.

I gassed the Chevy, bought some cigs, but no beers. I learned a lesson years ago about drinking and driving. I may drink a lot, but I get someone else to drive if I have to go someplace after drinking. When you almost die from too much booze it gives you a wake-up call. I woke up, and lost my wife. It doesn't bother me anymore, 'cause we weren't going anywhere anyway.

I know the route to Cyprus. The road will be a windy one-lane. The countryside is beautiful. The route I chose to drive

will take me by one of the hangouts I used to go to when I
was a kid. As I approach I get a little nostalgic, but that feeling vanishes quickly. The place is the pits! The Venticello
Resort has been taken over by a bunch of religious groups. As
I drive through the area, my stomach has a huge ache in it.
Every year for thirteen years my family came to this Italian
resort to spend part of each summer. Back then we didn't have
to put up with all this discrimination bullshit. Each nationality
had its own playground. The Jews had several places, the Pols
had a spot, and the Italians had three resorts in the Cascades.
Everyone was happy. I had a ton of Jewish and Polish friends.
We all raised hell and got drunk together during the summer.
Most of the time we only saw each other in the summers
because we lived in different areas of New York. It's tough to
find your own neighborhood in the city, let alone someone
else's. In those days I had some sweet Jewish girlfriends. I
had fun! Well so much for that, but it is nice to reminisce. My
dad will be pissed when I tell him that holy-rollers took over
the place. The reminiscing lasted half way to Cyprus. I had
better think of what to say and do instead of thinking about
when I was a kid in the mountains. I am approaching Cyprus.
The address indicates that the house is located on the main
drag of town. The village isn't too big, so I figure I can spot it
easily.

I drive slowly until I reach 458 S. Main, the address Bill
got from his records. The house is a typical two-story with a
small yard in front. It's a neat place, but the roof looks a little
ragged. I drive up the street to a supermarket and turn around.
I drive back to 458 S. Main and park in front. I still don't take
any chances so I park the car pointing out. As I walk up the
driveway to the front door I spot a pick-up parked in the
driveway. It isn't noticeable from the road. Before I knock on
the door I take a sneak peek at the truck. A quick glance
reveals a parking sticker in the left rear corner of the back
window. It is a horseman's sticker to Wildwood Racetrack.

Bill didn't tell me that Jacob's sister is related to the track in any way. I walk back around to the front door and ring the bell. I hear rustling in the background. I got good ears when I need them, so the next event is not totally unexpected. The door opens, and a slightly- built lady with blonde hair stands in front of me. I suspect she is about thirty-five years old.

"We don't want any, if you're selling something," she says curtly.

"I'm not selling Mrs. Lockhart. I'm here to ask you a couple of questions about Bret." That stops her.

"I don't know where Bret is so you're wasting your time and mine," she says, then tries to slam the door in my face. I told you I am ready for this. I put the old foot in the door and flash the credentials, which I don't like to use. She looks at the ID, then, releases the door.

"What do you want with Bret. He didn't do anything wrong."

"I don't suspect that Bret did anything wrong, Ms. Lockhart, but I need to find him. I think he is in danger. Plus, he can answer some difficult questions for me. By the way, do you race horses too?" I ask.

"No, I don't, I'm a ....," then catches herself.

"Then that isn't your truck in the driveway, is it Ms. Lockhart?"

She knows she is trapped and gives in.

"No, that's not my truck," she admits.

"Then whose truck is it, Ms. Lockhart?"

She tries to say something, but can't get it out. She breaks down and starts sobbing, uncontrollably. "He's upstairs," she says. "He's real bad mister, can you help him?" came the cry for help. I rush by her and leap up the stairs, the thirty-eight handy in case he is needed. I walk in the first room on the left and see him, that is, what was left of him. The pictures that Bill showed me of Bret Jacobs do not resemble the person who lies in front of me. Jacobs is covered with blood and

77

disheveled. He is barely sitting up in a large bed. The sister follows me in the room. Jacob looks at me with a blank expression. I look at Susan Lockhart. My eyes tell her what I want.

"He stumbled in here late last night. I don't see how he drove the truck to the house. He's a tough guy, but ….." she starts to cry again.

"Susan, may I call you Susan?" I ask. She nods through the tears. "Tell me what Bret said to you when he arrived looking like this? Try to be as specific as possible. I need to hear every little blurb, even if it wasn't coherent," I persist. She composes herself.

"I heard a noise at the front door. I thought it was some kids playing tricks or something, then I hear a moan. I rushed to the door and opened it to find Bret lying there. No telling how long he had been there or how long it took him to get from the truck to the house. I yelled for my son, Jacob, to help me. Jacob is nine years old and loves Bret. It is difficult for Jacob to see his uncle in that condition. Bret has been a father to him since my husband ran off with a stripper, seven years ago. We carried Bret upstairs and dabbed some of the blood off of him, but he is too hurt to move again. I may of hurt him carrying him upstairs, but I couldn't leave him in the doorway. He passed out and slept until a couple of hours ago. I didn't know what to do or who to call. I could have called Judy, but I don't much care for her attitude, then you came. Bret was just starting to get his senses when you came to the door," she explains. She looked exhausted. I imagine she didn't sleep well, not knowing the seriousness of her brother's condition. I give her a smile. She returns a faint one. I walk to Bret. Little Jacob is close by.

"Please help him, mister. I love Uncle Bret. Who would want to hurt him?" he asks mournfully. I can't say a word.

"Hush Jacob, let the man think. He says he is here to help Uncle Bret. He's a cop, so let him be." I look at Bret to see if I can talk to him. I can't. I reach for the cell phone. I ask the two of them to leave the room while I make a call. Susan looks a little perturbed at that request, but she complies. With the coast clear I call Bill.

I catch Bill at home.

"Bill, Sal here. I need some help. Can you get that retired Doc who put me back together?"

"I think so Sal. What is the deal, what did you find?"

" I found Bret Jacobs at his sister's house. He's in bad shape and needs attention, not the kind of attention that will be publicized. Will he make a house call for us? Bret needs a lot of help."

"I'll call him and buzz you back," he says. It only took five minutes.

"He's a little squeamish, but he'll come. He wants you to understand that if the man is hurt seriously, he will take him to a hospital. Do you agree?' he asks. I did; then told him to hurry. He told me to keep him comfortable until they get there in two hours. I agree, then I tell Susan and Jacob what is happening. I also tell them that I don't want either of them to leave the house or talk on the phone until help arrives. If Jacob wants to sit with his uncle and keep him company, that's okay, just don't touch or move him. If he talks, come and get me. They understand. I need a cig and brewski, but realize that a cigarette will have to do.

I decide to go to the back porch and light up. The door opens again and Susan appears. In this light she is an attractive woman with basic features. A little TLC and makeup would make her a killer. I guess she is living hand-to-mouth based on the look of things. She speaks.

"I don't know who you are mister, I didn't get a clear look at the name you flashed me, but if you wanted to hurt Bret, you could have pushed by me real easy. So I guess, what I'm saying, is that Jacob and I have got to trust you," she explains. I nod but am in no mood for small talk. It is apparent to me that Jacobs was intended to be the next victim, but somehow managed to escape the wrath of the killers. I did not intend to tell Susan Lockhart that someone tried to kill her brother. I made small talk instead.

"You can trust me Susan. Bret doesn't know me but knows of me. I'll explain when my people get here," She has that blank expression on her face, again.

'Do you want a snack while you wait?" she asks. I'm starving. I have a bad habit of not eating when I'm on a tough case. I drink too much and eat too little, not a good combo.

"Thank you, that would be nice," lying through my teeth. It's a wonder she didn't hear my stomach answer for me. I follow her into the kitchen after I put the cig out.

"Salami and cheese all right?" I nod. Mercy, I'm out in nowhere and I get salami. Can't beat it. "I work at a deli, so I get all this good meat and bread at half price. It fills us up. I don't make a lot of money and Jacob's dad doesn't send money anymore, so every little bit helps. Jacob loves the bread," she continues. "Will you tell me what is going on, mist....oh I forgot your name," she stammers.

"Sal, Sal Domino," as I help her with her memory.

"Yes, Sal-that's right. Will you tell me what is going on? I've been around the racing business long enough with Bret to know that things happen from time to time that aren't on the up-and- up. Am I right in assuming that?" I am trying to delay giving her any more details until Doc and Bill arrive.

"There is a possibility that Bret knows something that will help me solve a case, and Bret probably got hurt because of what he knows. I did not reach him in time. Bret is not in any trouble with the law, but with some unscrupulous characters." She digests what I tell her.

"Does this have to do with the fixed race and murders at Wildwood?" I nod, without wanting to talk anymore. She persists.

"Do you know who did this horrible thing to my brother?"

I shake my head, still not wanting to talk. "Why won't you talk to me? My brother is laying up there with the shit beat outa him, and you clam up," she argues.

"Susan; you will find out in due time. Now listen to me. I have to attend to Bret's injuries first, then I have to talk to him, if he's able. I will listen to what he tells me, then, I may be able to tell you. You must understand this. I can only do this one step at a time. I am not deliberately trying to evade your questions, but there is a process I must follow. Do you understand that? As long as I am here, no harm will come to you, Bret, or Jacob. Now, say you understand that, please?" I ask again, determined to get the answer. She nods but keeps her head down trying to fight back the tears.

CHAPTER NINE

We do not speak until I finish the sandwich, chips and milk. Her head is still down. I return outside to finish my smoke. The salami is a good brand and the cig tastes good after lunch. I am finishing the second cig, when I hear a car, it's Bill and the Doc in Ellie's Caddy. Bill must have pleaded his case to get the Caddy. The beater wouldn't have made the trip. I signal them to come around back. The Doc looks at me and I know he wants to ask me why I'm not in bed. I think the Doc is catching on to how Bill and I do business and the kind of assholes we are dealing with. Bill must have briefed him on the drive up. The Doc looks energetic, as if he would do anything to save mankind. I wonder how he would feel if I shot and killed one of 'mankind'. I show them the way to the room. Susan and Jacob look at us as if we are the FBI or something. We arrive at the room and Doc takes a quick look at Bret.

"Sal and Bill stay with me. Young lady, I notice a bathroom up here. Bring me with two large pots of hot water and some clean towels, I mean clean, preferably ones that have not been used yet. Young man, help your mother carry the water. Gentlemen, help me get this man's clothes off. Everyone to work, let's go," he commands!

Bret wakes, but is incoherent. We are attempting to get his clothes off and Doc is very carefully giving directions. He keeps mumbling to himself that this man should be in the hospital, but continues to give orders. He makes it clear that there is no way to determine the severity of the man's injuries under these circumstances. We will follow his directions to the letter. We start at the feet where the boots are soiled beyond repair.

The left boot comes off easy, but the right one is stubborn. There is a reason for that; the right foot is broken. Doc orders Susan to find a sharp pair of scissors. We are silent as Susan searches for the scissors. She appears with a long, somewhat, rusty pair she finds in the garage. They will have to do. Bill offers a sharp switchblade he keeps in the car for Ellie. Doc likes that idea better and sends Bill for the knife.

We start to cut into the boot. Bret grimaces a little but hangs in there. The boot is cut down each side until the foot is exposed. It is swollen and when new air gets to the foot, it swells even more. Doc explains to Bret that there will be some pain and he will have to grit his teeth. Doc will not give him a pain shot until he finishes his examination. The boot is worked free from the foot, and with one big yank, the foot is free. Bret shrieks with pain but calms down after the initial shock. Susan asks Doc if Bret can have a shot of whiskey, the Doc nixes it. Both feet are free and the only serious wound is the broken right ankle. The socks are cut off. His pants are cut up both sides of the leg. His belt is loosened and after rolling him to one side, can be taken off. The remaining top part of the pants is cut and the pants fold out. After rolling him over again, the pants are worked out from under Bret. He didn't shriek this time. The shirt is cut up each side and removed the same way as the pants, by being folded out. The roll over process works again as the shirt comes off. Bret is in his underwear and Susan and Jacob are asked to leave the room. The final strip of the patient is completed as the underwear is removed by cutting it up the middle. Bret lays nude, in front of us. His body is a mangled wreck. I will be interested to hear his story. It almost looks as if he were thrown from a car at high speed. We'll see. Doc does his thing. Besides the broken ankle, he has a broken shoulder; in two places, a severe laceration on his right thigh that will need stitches, five broken ribs, a concussion, along with several bumps, scratches and bruises. How in the hell did he survive, let alone manage to get home? Did someone help him? Doc proceeds to clean the patient with the two pots of water that Susan and Jacob brought. We need more water before Doc is finished. After two long hours, Bret looks better, physically. The foot is packed in ice, and his ribs are taped like a mummy, like mine are. The shoulder is separated, but not broken. The collarbone is broken. Doc makes a sling out of an old sheet and straps Bret into it to keep the blade and shoulder from moving.

Doc has some novocaine in his bag. He gives Bret a shot then closes the thigh wound using fifty stitches. The cuts on his head are bandaged. Doc thinks the concussion will be okay with rest. Finally, Doc sets the ankle and puts the foot in a plastic cast. He tells us that the foot should be set professionally, when the patient is better. Doc covers Bret with a large sheet. He then gives Bret some pain medication and puts some sleeping pills and more pain pills for Bret to take later. Finally, he speaks to us.

"Bill, gather everyone in the downstairs parlor. I want to talk to all the parties involved," Bill does as he is told. We wait for the Doc to say his piece. He speaks to Susan and Jacob first.

"This guy is extremely lucky. He has suffered some horrible damage to his body. He's a strong man, and it is that strength and a will to live that will help him beat the odds. He is not out of the woods by any stretch of the imagination, but with constant care and supervision, he should recover from his injuries. He will need help to use the bathroom and to do basic cleansing. You will want to pick up a set of crutches. Feed him regularly, soft food to begin with. I notice there is some damage to his jaw, but nothing is broken. The pills are here to use for his comfort, use them wisely. If he takes a turn for the worse, he must go to a hospital. Is that clear?" They both nod. "Are there any questions from either of you?" They shake their heads, indicating they understand the instructions. . Doc looks at Jacob and asks "young man, is this your Daddy?"

"No sir, he is my uncle." says Jacob, his voice shivering.

"Then you give him all the care he needs, okay?" Jacob nods then buries his head in his mother's shoulder and cries. Susan smiles at the Doc.

"You two go sit with the patient while I have a talk with these fine gentlemen here. Thank you for the help, you both did a great job." They follow Doc's orders and leave. Susan glances at me and I give a nod of approval. She's a strong woman. We wait until the two of them have gone upstairs, then Doc speaks.

"Gentlemen, this is a travesty. I do not know what the hell is going on with all this violence, but you are both dealing with some dangerous people. After I treated Sal, I called a friend of mine in the coroner's office. I called saying that I am a family friend and want to know about the young man's death. I believe it was the Olmstead body. They described a horrible death. This man wasn't just stabbed, but in a scientific way. It was done in a way that would allow him to feel his death before he finally succumbed, just a terrible way to die. As I was talking, we got into the other case. Since we are doctors, we talked about the other man's death, off the record of course. The black man was partially strangled, losing oxygen, before his neck was broken. This means that the man suffered before they finally put him to death, by breaking his neck. These murders are not only brutal; they are against all dignity of man. Most people choose to die quickly, not in the painful way these men died. We are dealing with devoids, people who are lacking in human emotion. They don't care what, how, where, or when a person is killed. The young man upstairs is fortunate. His story is more interesting, since he will probably live to tell about it. He was tortured before, what the murderers thought, would be imminent death. He was hit across the shoulder to cause the break or separation. The other one is hit also, but there is only superficial damage. The laceration on the thigh is a careful incision to allow for slow seepage of blood, making the person die of a loss of blood. The foot was placed in some type of vice; then the ankle snapped like a twig. His head has been beaten with a padded instrument to cause permanent brain damage. After all of this, the man was either run over by a car or thrown off a cliff. We are talking about a rugged man up there, one whose will to live blocked out all the pain he could stand. He is, and probably will make it, because of that will. Gentlemen; I close with this thought and possible advice to you. Get some heavy hitters in here to combat these people, before they get you all. These are unscrupulous people who will stop at nothing to get what they want. Sal, for some reason, you are still alive. I would not push it. They could have killed you any time. Be careful, and cover your tracks, and trust no one. Both of you are intelligent men. Do you understand what I'm telling you," as he finally finishes.

For the first time in recent memory I am without words. I look at Bill, who is as white as a sheet. We are dealing with professional monsters.

"Sal, take responsibility for that man's care and treatment. I will give you and Bill my private phone number. I spend my days reading medical journals. If I can be of help by telephone I will, but I prefer not to see that man again. If he takes a turn for the worse, you know what to do. Bill, take me home, I've had enough for one day. Good night," he says as he waves walking out the door. Ellie's Caddy looks a whole lot better than Bill's beater.

I'm alone. I hear something. What's that noise? Oh God, I need a brewski. I want a cig . . . oh, where is my lighter. I want Gretchen, no Mary. Domino, get a grip. I hear a noise again. It's Susan walking to the back porch to join me in a smoke. "Want a beer", I hear. Hell yes, I want a beer.

"Thank you so much," I say, politely, as I guzzle the brew

"Does that mean you need another?" she asks. I nod, embarrassed.

She brought two more, apparently during my embarrassment she gulped hers. Oh, well. Five beers each loosened us up a bit. The situation has not been easy. I will break one of my cardinal rules, and drive the Chevy home after I have been drinking. I make sure she is safely in the house before I drive off. The drive is one of the worst moments of my life. I commit another sin, by drinking on the way home. I smoke, drink and listen to some smooth jazz on my way to Bill's house. At least, if they get me now, I won't feel shit. Let them have my sorry ass. I'm not worth a shit if I can't solve this case. Kill my ass, you scumbags! I yell it so loud, it sobers me up a little. I come to my senses as I drive into the city limits. It is only a short skip to Bill's house. I pull around back and notice a light on in his bedroom. Ellie is waiting for me, what a lady. When I open the door to the apartment, her light goes out. I throw my clothes off, and flop on the bed. I don't care what time I get up in the morning! I'm exhausted!

CHAPTER TEN

The morning brings a steady rain and I lie awake pondering what happened last night. I will call Susan to check on the patient. I need to speak to Bret as soon as possible. I stumble to the bathroom and take a whiz. The brewskis have taken their toll. I am very fortunate to have arrived home safely. I used poor judgment in driving and I'll try not to do that again. I throw on some clothes and walk to the main house. The smell of coffee arouses my senses. Ellie has some made, so I help myself and walk back to the apartment. As I stand on the porch smoking a cigarette, I go over what Doc said last night; he said 'bring in some heavy hitters'. That's what he said. I am a stubborn person. I told you from the get go that I like to work alone. That is not an ego thing, but a confidence thing. I work better by myself. In this case I have an ex-cop to get some info for me when needed. Bill has been an important ally in this case; however he has a job to do just taking care of that track during normal hours. I'm here on my own.

I have to call Mary and explain why I didn't answer last night. I'll shower, then call her before I go to the track. The shower feels wonderful. I wonder when Bret Jacobs will be able to take a shower again? Most things we take for granted in this world; and a hot shower is one of them. I shave. The tender area around my jaw feels almost normal. I need a haircut; the locks are getting rather shaggy. I put on the clothes Ellie gave me. If I am going to be here for a while, I should buy some decent togs. The cell phone works and I call Mary. I let it ring once. I will have to wait for her to call from the pay phone. The wait only takes twenty minutes. I feel the wrath.

"Where have you been," she screams. "I have been waiting

for hours to hear from you. What is going on up there? Are you okay?" She continues with the questions.

"Sorry about the missing person act. I was detained and couldn't use the phone. Bill Beane and I were in a situation where I could not use a phone. Do you have any info I can use? Are you being careful?"

"Yes, I got something. I called the Wagering Facilitator, as you suggested. They have printed a report and will mail it ASAP. They have been doing their own due diligence. The man at Wildwood told me that there are 4,367 places that took bets on Wildwood on the night in question. The network is astronomical!" she explains. "Our office has tried to alert all the outlets to be on the lookout for people cashing winning tickets, but it seems the culprits have cashed most of them already. Also, an unidentified man cashed tickets worth more that $300,000 in the city. There is a man in the upstate who cashed $400,000. Some of the outlets still have not reported. I'm sure the amount of winning dollars will be staggering. I'll keep working on it," she explains further.

"Good job, Mary. Have you given any thought to who might be our leak at the agency?" Silence.

"No, I'm afraid to speak to anyone, except Jack. He sends his regards as usual. He doesn't want to hear from you until you've nabbed these guys, he says. Can you come down for a visit, I miss you." Do I hear right, or am I deranged? She misses me! I wonder how Gretchen will feel about that?

"No, I can't break away, but the thought is inviting. Thanks for thinking of me. It has been rather lonely up here," lying through my teeth. " I'll be in touch."

"Okay, but be careful and watch your drinking."

The conversation is enlightening. Several hundred thousand dollars have been cashed, just the tip of the iceberg. The final tote board results will be coming in soon. I need to get to the track and visit Butch Green. I wonder how he feels after I gave him that shot to the ribs?

I drive to the guard gate, and the same guard is on duty today. He nods at the guard shack and I drive right on through. It is right before the weekend and the horsemen are positioning their horses for the weekend race cards. Wildwood will race on Friday, Saturday and Sunday afternoons. This will allow bettors throughout the country to place bets on the Wildwood races. I don't think there will be a problem, but this will give me a chance to snoop around and see who's in action and who bets heavily. It may not give me any leads, but just being around the action will give me some insights Bill is waiting for me.

"It wasn't a nice night, was it?" I shake my head no.

"The barn area is talking all about how you slugged Butch Green. He is not very well liked because of his big mouth. Are you going to pay him a visit?" Bill asks. I nod again, I'm not in a talkative mood this morning. I pat him on the shoulder as I climb back in the Chevy. Barn X is the next stop. As I drive to the barn I see Horseshoe with his shoeing kit, walking the barns trying to hustle business. He catches my eye and gives me a sly grin as if to say 'go screw yourself copper.' He will come through in the end. I make the same U-turn at the top of the hill as I did before. I park on the downhill and get out of the Chevy. The last time I did this I was a hurtin' gator, but I am doing better today. Besides, I may have to cuff Green again. I hear his high-pitched voice, what an annoying little jerk he is. I may cuff him, just on general principles. I know he sees me but chooses to ignore me. I stand in his line of sight just to rattle his skinny ass. I'll stay there until he acknowledges me.

"What do you want today copper? Do you want to slug me again?" he asks, sarcastically. Not a bad idea, I think. "I told you all I'm gonna tell, now why don't you go on outa here," he says bravely in front of his staff. Mr. tough guy, what a joke!

"Green, I don't want to waste my energy by slugging you again, even though you deserve it. And I'm going to ask you as many questions as I want to, that's my job. I know you had something to do with that race, and I'm going to prove it," I say it loud and clear enough for all to hear. "Now, point me in the direction of Jumpin' Jimmy."

"Billy, show this guy where Jimmy is. Stay with him the whole time. If you move, you're fired," he yells. I follow Billy.

"You let him talk to you that way, Billy?" trying to get a rise out of him.

"Most of the time he's okay. When he drinks people stay out of his way. I just ignore him and he don't bother me none," Billy says nonchalantly. " I only work here because I get paid more than any other trainer-driver on this track. I can put up with the shit sometimes," he explains. "Here's Jimmy." Jimmy looks very lively this morning. I wonder what they feed these animals? His skin is shiny and the hooves are neat and painted. Must be Horseshoe's work. His big mitts have a calling in life.

"Nice horse Billy, do you take care of him?" I try and bait him. No go.

"Nah, this here's Horseshoe's side to groom. I got the other side of the barn," he explains.

"Boy, is he in good shape, a real pretty horse. Is he very old Billy?" I ask.

"This nag is eleven years old. He looks as if he is getting younger instead of older. Some horses will do that. Some mature in their later years," he explains, further. "His personality has changed too," adds Billy. Billy didn't know it but he confirmed what I suspected. This is not Jimmy! The question that remains is who is this horse? We walk away.

"Thanks for the info, you have been a real help." Boy, is that an understatement!

"Hey Green, give this boy a raise, he deserves it," I yell at Butch. He mumbles under his breath, 'go screw yourself copper.' Nice guy!

It is time to talk to the judges again. Boy, I don't want to go there, Masterson is such a jerk. I'll rile his ass again, watch me. I drive to the judges' office from Butch's barn. The race department is going nuts trying to fill races in advance. They try and stay three or four days ahead. I walk to Masterson's cubicle, and peek in.

"Peek-a-boo," I yell in my most obnoxious tone, then spot the judge. "Is anybody home?" I am a true ball-breaker. He ignores me.

I wait in the doorway until I am recognized.

"What do you want Domino?" he asks impatiently

"Judge, who is your paddock judge? I need to talk with him for a second. Is he around?"

"She, Domino, she. The Paddock Judge is a woman. What do you want to talk to her about?"

"Now, judge. Do I get in your personal business? I may want to ask her out for a beer," I say, playfully.

"You're a total asshole, Domino. There isn't a woman alive who would be caught dead with your sorry ass," he mocks me. "She's in the race office, go find her yourself." Why is everyone so nasty to me today? Maybe the judge is right, maybe I am an asshole. Screw'm all!

I find her. Forget about taking her out for a beer, she is a beast. I have much better taste, despite what the judge thinks. "Excuse me, ma'am, are you the Paddock judge?" I ask in my sweetest tone.

"Why, yes I am. My name is Jill Jones, and who are you?" Please lady don't flirt with me, I can't take it.

"Sal Domino, from the NGPA. Could I ask you a question or two, if you have a moment?" This is my sweetest tone possible.

"Of course, Mr. Domino, right this way," She points to her left. "What can I do for you?"

"Jill, will you tell me your procedures on inspecting a horse tattoo when that horse is in the paddock before a race?"

"Sure. Each horse has to be in the stall that designates what race position he or she, has drawn, usually numbers 1-8. The stall also has to designate the race number in which the horse is competing. I have a complete list of each horse and each race. They must match up correctly. I then go around before each race and check the horses' markings and tattoos. To check the tattoos I raise the top lip and read off a number that is tattooed there. That number must correspond to the number on the registration form. If there is a difference, then the horse is immediately scratched from that race. The next day, the trainer of the horse will go in front of a panel of judges to clarify the mistake. Does that answer your question, Mr. Domino?" Boy, I can get used to this Mr. Domino thing. She is very thorough, but I think the race fixers got one by her. I can't figure out how they switched the horses and got by this process.

"Jill, that is a perfect explanation. I didn't know the intricacies of the job. In your opinion, is there a way where a horse can be switched during this process, or something being changed during the same process?"

"Of course, Mr. Domino, there can be mistakes on the part of the trainer. A groom can bring the wrong horse to the paddock, but that happens infrequently. As for changing anything, I have been a paddock judge for twelve years, and I have not heard of a mistake that could be labeled intentional" I thank her and beat it out of there. I didn't want to see Masterson again. I go back to Bill's office.

We decide to venture to the track kitchen again. Ellie had to leave the house early this morning and won't be back until later, so Bill is going to hang around the track for the afternoon. I tell him the treat is on me. We order a baked chicken, salad and coke for only $2.75. We settle in a corner and eat lunch, great stuff. I tell him about the conversations that I had earlier. After lunch I will call Susan Lockhart to check on the condition of Bret. We walk back to the shack, and I make the call.

"Hello, Lockhart residence," the voice says. It's a woman.

"Susan, this is Sal Domino. How is Bret this morning?"

"Hello Sal. I'm glad you called. Bret is resting comfortably, but is in a lot of pain. I'm giving him the pain medication that Doc left. It settles him down and puts him to sleep. He wants to talk to you. He is not very strong, but he wants to get what happened to him off his mind. He won't mention anything to me. He keeps asking for you. Will you come right over?" she pleads.

"I'll be there in two hours. Don't tell anyone I called." She agrees.

I tell Bill where I'll be. I check the cell phone and find it charged and ready. I drive out the guard gate and get a nod from the old-timer manning it. I gas up the Chevy and buy a pack of cigs. My belly is full and so is the Chevy's, we are on our way.

CHAPTER ELEVEN

I take a different road to Cyprus this time. If I go by the Venticello Resort I'll be sick. I can't see that place in the condition it is in, I prefer to remember the good times. Instead, on this route I'll pass by The Everglades, a Jewish hangout. One summer I met Donna, a little Jewish girl. She had just turned sixteen and her Dad threw this amazing shindig for her. When the Jews throw a party they spare no expense, especially when the Jewish princess turns sixteen. We played around that summer, but never got serious. The Venticello was near the Everglades, so we snuck out to drink her dad's vodka and feel each other up. She liked to play that way. Well, just after her sixteenth birthday, one night we had just a little too much vodka and played a little too much. We went 'all the way.' For us, it was a big deal. The first time is always a big deal. We sweated it out until she got her period, then we were cool about it. When I was seventeen and eighteen, I screwed my brains out every summer. I even worked part time at the Everglades when I was eighteen. Those days I will never forget. Growing up in the mountains was great! The Everglades is just around the next corner. Wow, another religious community. At least the place is respectable and cleaner than the Venticello. I guess the mountains aren't what they used to be, I just have the memories.

It's ten more miles to Cyprus. I switch to a jazz tape because I lost the jazz station on the radio. I think about what Bret is going to tell me. Cyprus City limits straight ahead. I find the street, pull up to the supermarket and turn around. I drive back to the house and park on the street, pointing out. I get out of the Chevy and lock the money in tight. I check for the cigs, phone and the thirty-eight. All is well. I walk around back and see the truck still in the same location. I knock on the back door. Susan is waiting, and immediately opens the door. I nod and try to go upstairs. She stops me by grabbing my jacket and asks if I want anything to drink. I shake my head no and continue up the stairs. She is persistent.

"Will you wait a minute, please!" she yells. I stop. "I want to be in on the conversation, Sal," she yells, again. I walk down the stairs.

"Susan, you can't be there. The description of the details will be too much for you. I will fill you in on everything when the time is right. Didn't I tell you that?" She bows her head and nods. She runs to me and buries her face on my chest. Life's a bitch. She's lost, broke and has a screwed-up brother. I move her toward a chair and comfort her for a second. When the time comes for me to go, I get up and quietly walk away. I climb the stairs two at a time. I am anxious. Bret snaps awake when he sees me.

"You Domino?" I nod. He motions me to a chair by his bed. I sit and wait. I don't need to take any notes. I am able to memorize everything verbatim, as I long as I concentrate. He starts.

"Susan and Jacob won't be here, will they?" I shake my head.

"Susan says you are some kind of cop, is that right?" I nod again. He is resting between sentences. I admire the man for surviving.

"What I'm going to tell you will not leave this room, got it Domino? If you get these guys you will have to kill them, because that is the only way they will go. I'm not going to testify against anyone. Can you agree to that?" I nod. "Do you want to take notes?" I shake my head.

"I will have to rest from time to time. Are you responsible for saving my life and cleaning me up?" I remember what the Doc said about accountability and I nod again. "Well, maybe I will make it or maybe not, but I will tell you what happened to me. I have got to tell someone." He takes a deep breath, cringes, and begins to tell the story from hell.

"I am entered in the race driving one of Judy's horses. Judy is a screwed-up gal, but she trains her horses well and gives me a shot to win every time I'm in the sulky. I notice that the paddock is unusually quiet this afternoon. Most of the time you can hear Butch and that high voice of his carrying on, but not today. I didn't think anything so I went about my business. I am driving six horses that afternoon, and I am busy warming up horses all day. You can warm up horses on the off races. I don't bet a lot, so I didn't look at the tote boards. I warm up Slow Poke, and she is a terror to hold on to. I feel my chances in that race are great. Slow Poke is a sore pacer, but when she feels good she'll tear the reins right out of your hand. That is the way she felt that day. That was one race I didn't worry about winning because I have beaten most of these horses several times. (He rests) Except, something odd is happening. Jumpin' Jimmy is also warming up. Jimmy has no heart and just races to get a check. Butch Green does all he can, but the animal is all raced out-but not tonight. Jimmy warms up great. He almost didn't look like the same Jimmy. Turns out I was right. The more I look at Jimmy, the more I am convinced that this is a different horse. Of course, he looks identical to Jimmy, but there is something about his gait. You can tell when you have been around horses as long as I have. It was time for the race. This is the first time I look at the tote board. The numbers that are showing are huge. I know the track is simulcasting races nationally, but we never have this much money in the pools. (He rests). The paddock is silent. The paddock is never silent. I say to myself, I better watch my ass in this race. Something is going down and it has to do with Jumpin' Jimmy. The starter calls for the horses and I go to the gate. I am slot #2; Jimmy is slot #7; Paul is in slot #8. Paul and I are favorites, as we should be, because we have the best horses that day. The race starts and Jimmy, with Butch in the sulky, breaks from the gate well. The Jimmy I know never breaks that well. I look to my right and let them go while tucking in along the rail. Normally, that is a good position for me because I can swing down the stretch and outpace everyone to the wire, but not tonight. I see Paul's horse break stride, then Jimmy takes the lead with Butch in the sulky, just sitting there. We turn for home and I have a ton of horse left to finish the race, except two horses are in front of me and will not let me go through on the rail. They are not trying to win the race but they are sure as shit stopping me from winning. I yell at the top of my lungs, but to no avail. I am stuck behind these assholes with nowhere to go. I was set up, big time. (He rests). I jog Slow Poke back to the paddock and look at Judy. She knows something is fishy. There is one race left but I'm not driving in it. The judges are calling for me, but I get the hell out of there. I didn't wait for the prices or talk to anyone, I book from the track. As I am leaving I pass Butch Green. He has a big smile on his face. I tell him I was going to 'kick his ass and steal that horse because it sure as shit isn't Jimmy'. I am furious. I drive to a joint and call Judy on her cell phone. I tell her that I am going to lay low for a while, until the shit clears.

   I hide for a couple of days but as I was on my way to my sister's some guy in a Cadillac cuts me off the road. Some animal clubs me over the head with a sort of pillow, except it is hard. The blow didn't hurt that much but it sure messes up my brain. (He rests). From here on out it gets kinda fuzzy. (I nod) I wake up, blindfolded, in an old barn somewhere out in the country, it smells like cows. I'm tied to a chair and placed in the center of a large floor. I'm still a little woozy. Someone speaks. "Hey tough guy. You picked the wrong punk to talk at tonight. Ya' see, Butch is a friend of ours. He helps us make a lot of money. He tells me that you figured out something. Gee, tough guy, you shouldn't have said anything," I feel a board or bat come down across my shoulders. I remember screaming in pain. Now it really gets woozy. (He rests) My head is hanging on my chest, but I see what happens next. Someone slides something and puts it by my feet. They put my foot in... it feels like a trap of some sort. I really lost it then. Someone picks up the trap and twists it until I feel my ankle snap. I scream so loud that I pass out. The next thing I remember; as I am in and out of consciousness, is riding in the back of a pick-up, bumping along some dirt road. I'm screaming in pain. I can't feel my shoulder or foot. I'm sore everywhere. I feel the truck stop. I am tossed down a ravine and bounce a long way until I come to rest at the bottom. I pass out again. I awake and pass out several times. I see blood everywhere. The next thing I remember is two guys trying to wake me, but I can't hear them. They give me water and I wake up. They say they are going to bring me to a hospital. I remember pleading with them not to. I mention the name of the grill where I was. I hear them talking. One of them gets my wallet out and looks at something as they talk it over. I feel like I'm pulled to a spot. I pass out again. I wake up in a bed of a truck, it's mine. I pass out again. The next thing I remember is being at Susan's front door. That's it."

I have a ton of questions for him, but now is not the time. He dozes off because of the effort. I don't know if I could have gone through what this man has. I'm a real smart-ass and a so-called tough guy, but I don't know if I'm that tough. I sit there and stare at him. There are some holes to fill in the story, but I think I can reason it out when I talk to him again. I decide to wait until he wakes up.

I walk down stairs and see Susan in the kitchen. She looks as if she is fixing supper. She sees me, but doesn't speak. I guess she is pissed because I was a little rough on her earlier. "Hi, Bret did fine with the story. He's resting now. He is truly a brave and tough man. I admire him for his sheer will to keep going, he refuses to die. We have to protect him because the people that did this to him, cannot find out he is alive or they will finish the job, and add some extra people too." She is a little unsteady on her feet.

She asks, "Will you stay for supper?"

I need to speak to Bret again so I will have to stay until he wakes up again.

"I would love to. Is there anything I can do to help?" I ask her knowing full well that I don't have a clue about a kitchen.

"Yes, you can," she acts surprised. "You can set the table. Here are the dishes and silverware. Set four places. We will remember Bret tonight by setting his place. Jacob usually sets the table, but he has football practice," she explains. I do as I am told. Jacob races in the house and asks about Uncle Bret. Susan does a good job with the explanation. We say a short prayer before a dinner of chipped beef, mashed potatoes, corn and gravy. I will get fat eating at this place. After dinner I sit outside and wait for the phone to ring, it's almost 6:00 p.m. The cigarette eases me as I sit comfortably in an old rocker. I am dozing off when the cell phone rings. I snap to attention.

"Go ahead, tell me what's up."

Mary says, "I hope you're okay, something isn't right with your voice. I know you too well, Sal Domino. Come clean with me."

"Not now, Mary. This is not the time, ease up on me will ya' " I don't want to be a hard ass, but her yelling at me is not what I need right now. If she knows me, then she'll pick up on that.

She continues, "I have tote printouts from all three tracks. Wildwood came first. I don't know how to read them. If I give them to someone else, the word may get out and the leak will find me. I don't want that. Sal, you have me paranoid." I want her to be paranoid, it will save her life. If she knows what I know about how these guys operate she would understand.

"That's great. Mary, I need you to come up here with me. You're no longer useful sitting in that office. If the leak moves closer to you, it can get dangerous. They probably know what you do, and it is a matter of time until they find out about our phone check in. Pack up all necessary material and clothes and head for the mountains. I want you to time it so you are on the road during the time we talk. At 6:00 p.m. call me from your cell phone and I will give you directions to where I'm staying. Tell Jack some story about a sick aunt, or something. If he asks about me, tell him I can take care of myself. Time it so they can't make a decision on you, say about 5:00 p.m. or so. Be packed and ready to go before then. If you have to, run out of the damn place. You got all that?" Silence.

"Okay Sal. I understand. This isn't like you. This case is supposed to be about race fixing but I know it goes much deeper than this. I will be ready to go. Don't worry about Jack, I can handle him. I will be on the road by 6:00 p.m., tomorrow, and I will call you when I'm out of the city. I haven't been to the mountains in a long time." I hope she doesn't think this will be a vacation!

I sit back down in the rocker, light a cig and begin to doze off again. Susan's at the door, I awaken from my slumber. "Jacob is asking a lot of questions about his uncle. I can only fib to him for so long. He wants to know who did this to him, and frankly Sal, so do I. My job is to make Bret comfortable, wash him and give him medicine. I am doing that to the best of my ability, I'm not a trained nurse, you know."

"Susan, you are doing a fabulous job. I'm sure the Doc would agree. When I crack the case we will give Bret the necessary professional attention he deserves, I promise." I mean every word.

"Our parents died when we were little kids and Bret has taken care of me for a long time. He tried to warn me about the jerk I was going to marry, but I didn't listen. I was a know-it-all, young and stupid. Before I knew it, I was pregnant with Jacob. The next few years were a blur. My husband fooled around on me. Bret beat the shit outa him one night when he saw him out with someone else. He left a short time after that. Bret sends me money so Jacob and I can have a decent life. Working in a deli doesn't cut it and I didn't make it through school. Bret bought this house for us and fixed it up. I owe my life to my brother Mr. Domino, and I will be there for him every step of the way. If he is crippled, I'll take care of him. Bret means the world to me, he's all I have besides my son. The Doc said that Bret has a will to live, well I have just as strong a will to keep him alive," she finishes. She's emotional. I think I admire her as much as I do Bret. The world is full of strong people, and these are just two of them. The more I think of these killers, the angrier I get. I have a reputation for keeping my cool but if the occasion should arise where I meet one of these assholes, I'll kill the son-of-a-bitch. I ask Susan to wake me when Bret can talk. She agrees and walks solemnly back to the kitchen, feeling better about herself. I doze off in the rocker again.

I almost fall out of the rocker. The sudden movement has me wide-awake. I light up, wishing I had a brewski to accompany the cig but I need to stay sharp. If I start drinking, my memory will leave me and then I won't be coherent enough to remember the conversation verbatim. I hear someone walking down the steps. It is 11:00 p.m. Susan peeks out the door and tells me Bret can speak again. I get off the rocker and head for the stairs.

I ease into the room, Bret sees me, and his eyes go up about a quarter inch. That is all the recognition I need. I wait for him.

"Did you get what I told you?" I nod

"Did I make any sense, I hope I didn't ramble," I nod.

"You don't talk much, do you Domino?" I have to answer this time.

" I talk too much, Bret. Sometimes I get in the sling because of it. This is your show, you don't need me to muddle the picture, until you are ready. Are you ready for me to ask some questions?" He nods.

"Did you see any of the people who clubbed you? Were there any distinguishing features on any of the guys that you can recall?" I give him time.

" No, the event took me by surprise. I didn't think anyone could have followed me. I had stayed low. I mean, the race just ended and I didn't stick around. Maybe someone was following me the whole time. I didn't know how many there were, I just know they were strong. I was half-conscious, but I remember them throwing me around like a rag doll. As for anything that stands out, I don't remember," he concludes.

"Did you smell anything, perfume, cologne?" He thinks.

"Yes, I can remember a smell of perfume. I am not thinking too clearly, but I figure it is men who slugged me. Maybe it was men, but the perfume smells like a woman. It could be some fag cologne from the city, but I remember the smell."

I remember a smell from my room too. "You said you couldn't see the area where they took you, but it did smell like cows. Are you sure of that?"

"Yes, I am. There is a distinct difference between the smell of horses and cows. I was taken to a farm, not a stable. I'm sure of that."

"Can you remember anything about the man who spoke to you, or the ones that hit you? Did you recognize any accents?"

"They are wise guys from the city, I feel it. I have shipped to the city to race many times, and I can recognize those tones, whether I am blindfolded or not. I only hear one voice. The guys that roughed me up didn't talk, they didn't have to." (He rests).

"You mention that two guys find you at the bottom of some valley. Do you know, or recognize them? It seems strange that these guys are there, did it seem they were hunting or something?"

"I don't know them from Adam. I was pretty out of it and in a great deal of pain. I guess I'm fortunate that they found me. I don't know if they were looking for me or if they were part of the gang," Bret explains.

"Were you able to detect an accent? Did you see or smell anything unusual?"

"No, I am in really bad shape when they find me, but I did notice one thing when they are lifting me. I am in and out of consciousness, so I can't really be sure, but I think I saw a horseshoe ring on one guy's finger. I can't be sure, I was all messed up."

"You're doing great, Bret, hang in there. I only have a few more questions. Let's talk about the race. You said you had a feeling in the paddock that something is going to go down. It is quiet, did you notice anything different, other than the silence?" He pauses.

"Horseshoe and Cotton are talking. You know them, don't you? (I nod). They are exchanging money, a lot of money. Now, neither of them has a pot to piss in or a window to throw it out of, but it looks as if they are handling a lot of dough. For what reason, I can't say. Did I say that Butch is quiet? (I nod). He's never quiet, that little prick runs his mouth from dawn to sunset," he continues.

I continue, "because of your knowledge of horses, you feel that Jumpin' Jimmy is a different horse. Describe why you feel that way?"

"I don't train or own horses, I just drive 'em. I drive thousands of horses a year, all over the country. You get to know what a horse is supposed to do or how a specific horse acts. I observe everything at a track I can get my eyes on. The only money I make is by driving. I give myself the best chance to win a race, based on my observations. There is absolutely no way the real Jimmy can race like that horse did the other afternoon, no way!" he shouts

(He rests). The noise brings Susan to the room. She peeks in the door, I whisper everything is okay, and she leaves.

"Bret, tell me about the guys who boxed you in? Do you

know them from the track? Are they trainers, owners, and drivers? Are they friends with Butch Green?" I ask a bunch of questions and wait, patiently.

"Jack Whalen is driving 'Fallin' Down', and Bill Freon is driving 'See ya' Later'. I know both of these horses. I drive 'See ya' Later' sometimes. Sal, you have to understand something about a fixed race. The horses do not run true to form because these guys are trying to get the right numbers on the board. They don't have a set combination that is supposed to win, instead they bet several combinations against the horses that are favored to win. They take care of the favorites on the track, by any means necessary, then the other numbers race to the wire. There is usually one strong horse that will win, and the rest of them will race for place and show. The key here is to not let the favorites in the money. The strong horse is Jimmy, but he really isn't Jimmy. That is why they made such a large score. Not only did they fix the race, but also they included a ringer. Do you know what a ringer is Sal? (I know, but I want him to tell me so I shake my head). A ringer is a horse that races in place of the horse that is entered to race. Somehow these guys got that horse past the race department, the paddock judge, the Vets, and the state judges. Sal, when that horse went by me on the track he is perfectly balanced. Remember, the horses in that race are bottom claimers, $2000-horses, and these horses have a lot of physical problems. The Jimmy that raced the other day is no $2000- claimer. I recognize a stakes horse when I see one, so did Paul. That is a classy animal that won that race, not a plug. No one was going to beat him. As for Whalen and Freon, their job was to prevent Paul and me from finishing in the top three. Paul recognizes what is happening and pulls his horse up, making her run. That makes Whalen's and Freon's job a lot easier. They only have me to worry about. They know my horse likes to race on the rail, so they put their asses right in front of me and I ain't goin' nowhere, and if I try, they'll put my ass over the rail."

"Whalen is a flunky. He never races his horses for the purse, he bets on them and makes money that way. I can't figure Freon, he's always been a solid guy. I know that Butch recruited these guys to help in that race. Green isn't too smart. I don't think he is the brains in this deal, but if you squeeze him, the little rat may squeal on the ones who are behind it."

Bret is exhausted. I call for Susan and she hustles up the stairs. We chat briefly then she gives Bret some pain medicine. He immediately falls asleep. I make my way to the porch and light a cig. It is the wee hours of the morning. Susan hasn't slept at all. She follows me to the porch with a glass of coke and I thank her. I feel her looking at me, and it isn't a little girl look either.

"Why don't you sleep here tonight? My bed is large enough for both of us."   I let her down gently.

"No thanks, I snore. But I will grab the couch if it's okay with you." She smiles and nods, maybe another time honey. I move to the couch. She comes into the room with a blanket and a pillow. I thank her and plop down. Before I can say Mary, Gretchen, Susan..... I'm asleep.

CHAPTER TWELVE

Jacob wakes and asks me why I have to sleep here and if his uncle is ok, a bunch of questions from a kid just rarin' to go in the morning. He bounces around from the shower to his bedroom to the kitchen, then kisses his mom goodbye and races out the door to go to school. What a whirlwind!

"Is he always like that?"

Susan smiles, "every day, he has a great deal of energy. Bret has a tough time keeping up with him. Do you want some coffee?" I nod. "Bret slept pretty comfortably, if that's possible. I think he feels better getting the story out of his head. You were very patient with him Sal, and I appreciate what you are doing for him."

" I told you he is a tough guy. I will not talk with him for a while. He must be nursed back to health. Susan, if his foot bothers him, call me and I'll come right over and take him to a doctor. But if at all possible, he should stay here. I don't want to move him because I don't want anyone to know that he is still alive, got it?" She nods and I leave.

I use the cell phone to call Bill, he answers.

"Wildwood security, Beane speaking."

"Pretty formal, Bill. Are you the secretary today as well as the chief?"

"Give me a break, Domino. I got a guy out this morning so I'm doubling up. What did you find out?"

"I'll brief you when I see you this morning. I have a hunch. Have your men on the lookout for a man wearing a horseshoe ring. It may be the break we are looking for. Someone found Jacobs at the bottom of a gully and I don't think it is a coincidence. I won't tell you any more about that because I don't want to influence your search. I need to speak to the judges again, God forbid. I'll be at the track in about an hour. Be prepared to have lunch somewhere, after I talk to them, so that I can brief you on the conversation I had with Jacobs." He agrees.

I smoke five cigarettes on the way to the track. I'm not paying attention to the roads I'm on and I come up on the Venticello again. It looks just as bad as it did the first time I saw it, ugh! I'm going to remember the Venticello as the summertime Mecca my parents took us to every summer. It's a shame what has happened to the mountains, a damn shame. The track sneaks up on me and I almost miss the turn. The guard flashes me in with a nod. I drive by the guard shack and continue to the judge's office. I know they are still there because of all the cars around. Maybe Judge Masterson is having a party. I park, lock the Chevy, put out the umpteenth cig and stride to the office. I knock this time, no games today. Masterson spots me, gives the flunkies the look and presto, we are alone.

"What is it, Domino?" he asks, impatiently.

"I need the answer to some questions, we can do this the easy way or the hard way. Which do you prefer?"

"Do I have a choice?" I shake my head, slowly. I'm trying to bait him.

"Have you interrogated Jacobs, Green, Whalen and Freon?"

"Why do you want to know? It is my investigation, what gives you the right to barge in here and obtain information that I might have?"

"Apparently we are not on the same page. Do you want to do this the easy or hard way? You don't have a choice, I thought I made that abundantly clear."

"Domino, you are a royal pain in the ass. Why are you badgering me like this? Give me some respect, will ya'. I deserve some respect!" he shouts. I wait, wait, he sighs.

"We can't find Jacobs. I know he has something to do with that race. He stiffed his horse," he explains. The judge continues, "we talked to Whalen and Freon and they tell us they are racing to win the race. They also say that they didn't know Jacobs is behind them trying to get through," he explains further.

Are they blind? I had to have this talk because I need to know if they know anything or not. Masterson isn't bullshitting me, they don't have a clue.

"Now that isn't hard, is it?" He's still steaming. I thank him and glide out of his office into the race office. The Race Secretary is a plump old guy who looks as if he's been around a track for thirty years. I walk over to him and introduce myself, without my card.

"I'm Sam Sparrow, how can I help you?"

"Can I see the registration papers on Jumpin' Jimmy?"

He balks,"can't give them to you sir, the trainer picked them up this morning, they are going to ship the horse out to race elsewhere. I suppose that is the best way to handle the horse because of his inconsistent showing. That last race came out of the blue and isn't a true indication of how the horse races," he explains.

I can't blame him, but is he in for a surprise when I find out who Jimmy really is. I thank him and bolt to the guard shack where Bill is waiting for me.

"Bill, where can we go to have a quiet lunch and not be recognized?"

He said, "no problem." and we head for the beater. I stop and check the locked Chevy. The beater actually runs fairly well, if you can withstand the fumes. I solve that by rolling down the window and lighting a cig. We have to drive about five miles until we come to a small café on the outskirts of town. We park, walk in and sit down. I order a coke and sandwich, as does Bill. I fill him in on the Jacob's story. I ask him about the horseshoe ring and he says no one has spotted one yet.

We return to the track. I want to watch some races this afternoon and wait for Mary to call, so I walk to the paddock, which is located on the opposite side of the grandstand, away from the public. That's a problem right there. The public doesn't trust these guys anyway and they can't see them either. Bill has given me a pass so I can walk around and look official. I don't want to look official so I hide the badge once I gain access to the paddock and mingle with the men and women there. You can't smoke in the paddock so I'm nervous already, I need a coke to settle me down. I have to go to the drivers' lounge for the coke where the mighty mouth Butch Green is holding court. Boy, he really is an annoying little shit. I eavesdrop until he spots me, then I quietly slip away. The conversation is reduced to a whisper. I know they are talking about me--who gives a shit? I'm after Green and he knows it. I'll bust his ass yet. I go through the entire paddock area, not wanting to talk to anyone, just observing. I want to get a better idea how the horses are prepared to race, when a race goes off, how it is run and the return trip to the paddock to unhook the equipment. It is interesting to watch. I spend almost three hours observing as much as I can, including watching the paddock judge go through the lip routine. Jill Jones is not bashful as she grabs the horse's mouth and gets a good look at the tattoo. If she has to, she'll yank the head upside down to do the job. Something is bothering me about this tattoo business. I can't put my finger on it.

Horses, grooms, trainers, drivers, owners, blacksmiths, vets, race and state personnel and whoever else has business in the paddock, come and go all afternoon. It is a job for the gate guard to keep up with it all. I can see a person sneaking in from time to time, but another horse-no way. I also watch the tote board. The people in the paddock have a disadvantage when it comes time to bet, they can't. There isn't a tote machine in the paddock and that means a runner has to go out and make a bet in the grandstand, then come all the way back to the paddock. That's why I see so much action going in and out, it is a policing nightmare. Bill recognizes that and lets the gamblers piss their money away if they want to. I see Bill a few times but he is doing his job, I don't bother him. I also don't want people seeing us talking. The afternoon goes by fast. I pick up some valuable info on race preparations and what it takes to keep this place running smoothly. I walk to my car and wait for Mary to call.

I drive out to Bill's place and park around back near the apartment. I sit on the porch smoking a cig. Ellie is not home. I get an uneasy feeling that I can't put my finger on. I have been watching my ass to look for tails. I haven't been putting the transparent tape on the door because I feel safe at Bill's. Maybe I better start doing that. The phone rings, it's Mary.

"Where are you and is anyone tailing you?"

"I'm about an hour away and no one is tailing me. I'm driving my sister's car to avoid that." Smart girl.

"Good, call me when you are in the city limits and watch your ass. Did you have any problems getting away?"

"No, I told Jack a line. See you soon."

CHAPTER THIRTEEN

When Bret described the action in the paddock that afternoon, he mentioned something about Cotton and Horseshoe holding a lot of cash. Now what would a couple of black guys who don't have anything be doing with that much cash? I found the cash in Cotton's room, but I don't dare search Horseshoe's room. I've got to go see Horseshoe again. I still have the papers that Bill gave me regarding the drug deal involving Horseshoe. I think it is time to use the leverage. I think there may be more money, too. If Horseshoe knows that Jimmy really isn't Jimmy, then what is keeping him alive?

The phone rings again, it's Mary. I give her directions to the house and wait. Bill drives up with Ellie behind him. I guess they went shopping. I fill Bill in on the details of Mary coming to visit and hope that Ellie can fit her in somewhere. She smiles at me. I suggest finding Mary a room of her own. Mary pulls in and parks by the Chevy. She's driving a Lincoln Navigator. Her sister must be doing okay. I can't even afford the tax on one of those things. Mary gets out and starts chatting to Ellie, ignoring me. Mary settles in then decides to acknowledge me with a peck on the cheek. We have a wonderful supper of stuffed chicken, baked potatoes, fresh green beans, salad and a bottle of wine. Ellie is gracious enough to buy beer for me. After dinner we chat about small stuff. I smoke a cig on the porch and leave the ladies to yakking. Bill follows me out.

"I saw you snooping around the paddock today. Did you see something of interest?"

"Nah, I was just goofin' around. I had to rile Green though. I like bustin' his balls. We have got to pin something

115

on him to make him talk. He's an arrogant little shit if I ever saw one. I got an idea. I need to see Horseshoe again. He's not going to be happy, but tough shit. I'm going to squeeze him about the money in the paddock. He's going to wonder how I got that info so I'll keep a tight line on him. I think he has some cash too. He knows about that horse, but he doesn't know how the switch was made. I'm going to have him show me Jumpin' Jimmy before they ship him out, if they haven't already. I'm going down there tonight Bill. I need to surprise him and I'm bringing my gun. Will you cover me with Mary? I don't want her to know where I'm going. If she beefs, have her look at those printouts until I get back. She has to be familiar with the betting patterns."

Bill cautions me, "You better watch your ass, Sal. If someone finds out you are there, you'll end up in the in field lake with cement feet and I'll never find your dago ass. Do you want me to tell Mary you're going to wear Rinker boots?" I shake my head and giggle. He continues, "I'll call the night guard and notify him you will be coming."

I'm gone. I don't know what I'm looking for. Is it Horseshoe's money or Cotton's? When I see the horse, what the hell am I gonna do? I don't know anything about horses or their lips or how they shit. I need to squeeze Horseshoe hard, real hard. I don't want to drive on the grounds so I park the Chevy on the side of the road, pointing in the right direction. I get out and lock the money up. The old-timer at the gate is watching me the whole time. I'm sure he's an ex-cop, so he'll figure it out. I walk up to the gate and he waves me through. Bill has a bunch of old ball-breakers as guards, but I bet they are efficient. I walk in the shadows to the Grooms' building. What a scary place it is at night. The windows are open and I hear loud noises. It appears there is a large card game going on. I wonder if Horseshoe is playing. I slip to the window where the voices are coming from, and look in. No one sees me. I don't see Horseshoe. I walk to the side entrance and ease in, quietly. I don't know which room is his, so I have to wait. If he is part of the card game he has to surface soon. I'm right, his big ass appears from the bathroom. I signal him. He sees me and is not too happy. He stalks to where I'm standing.

"We got business fella." He glares, I mean really glares at me.

"What you doing in my building copper? I oughta call the boys and have them whup up your white ass. This better be good." I wave the drug papers at him. He understands.

" I was wonderin' when you were goin' to call those in."

"It's time 'shoe. Let's go. Tell the boys you got a hot date or some bullshit like that." He laughs.

"Old Horseshoe ain't been with no gal in a long time, they nothin' but trouble. I'll tell them some story." I nod, keeping the thirty-eight handy. He comes back and signals us outside.

"Let's get this over copper, I don't want nothin' hangin' over my head. If I owe you, let old 'shoe pay up," he reasons. I lead the way, not afraid.

"We are going to barn X, 'shoe. I think you know what I'm looking for." He's mum. He takes the lead and finds a short cut to barn X. The climb up the hill to the barn is a little more treacherous at night.

"You better hope the horse is still there, they were going to ship it out to a farm," says 'shoe.

I'm praying. We walk to the side of the barn that Horseshoe grooms and in stall 28 is Jimmy, or whoever it is. I'm stuck, but I have to play the roll.

"Okay, now what copper. What you gonna do now? What you wanna' see? There's the horse, make a move."

"Listen 'shoe, I've got an idea. It may sound crazy, but I have to look at something."

"You wanna look at his dick or somethin', he ain't got no balls, he's gelded," describes Horseshoe. He gets to the point, doesn't he?

"No, I don't want to see that, but I do want to see the tattoo. I need your help." He laughs, then catches himself.

"You ain't never been around no horses, have you copper?"

I have, but not this close. My cases have always been from afar. I'm right in the shit now.

"I want you to hold the lip up and allow me to read the number. Can you do that?" He laughs again, this time not so loud.

"Okay, copper, I'll lift the lip. This ain't Jimmy, but no horse can get away from old 'shoe's grip," he says, confidently. Somehow, I believe him. He raises the lip. Jimmy or whoever, is pissed. He wants to sleep, not be messed with. I see the number and memorize it-4589766. I read it again so there will be no mistake. The tattoo looks legit. I nod to Horseshoe and he lets the lip down. The horse stomps to his feedbag and chomps down on some oats. I repeat the number, 4589766, got it. We start to walk back to the grooms' building. I need to surprise him about the money, but I have to time it right, better now than later.

"We have something else to discuss, Horseshoe." There's the glare again.

"Com'on copper, I did what you want, why you screw'n with me?" He's still glaring at me.

"I have some info that on the afternoon of the race, you and Cotton are playing with some large amounts of cash in the paddock." Now it's my turn to glare.

"You got it wrong copper, me and Cotton never had no cash."

I keep glaring at him, and wait, this time for a while. The big man is thinking. What is going through his brain? He's probably thinking about how his big ass is going to get ripped up in the big house. He shakes his head.

"Okay, copper, you win. I don't wanna go to the pen again. I'll tell you about it. Me and Cotton figure out that Jimmy ain't really Jimmy. So, Cotton goes and holds up Butch. Well, you can't screw with Butch, 'cause he's a crazy son-of-a-bitch. Butch is small but he has muscle behind him. They pay Cotton to keep his mouth shut. I don't go near Butch 'cause I work for him so they only deal with Cotton. The money flows in, but Cotton keeps it all. He buys all the cigarettes and booze, and bets for us too. I guess he messed up 'cause they broke his neck," he describes. Even the big man doesn't want to die. There is a pall over his black face.

"You got any of the cash?" I ask.

" Hell, no, I ain't got no cash, I'm poorer than a southern slave, honest copper, I don't got any," he pleads. He's scared. I believe him and leave.

"Hey, what about our deal?"

" Bill Beane will be in touch with you," I yell as I scoot away.

I hurry to the gate, wave at the guard and open the Chevy. I smoke a cig on the way to Bill's house. 4589766, that's the number.

I arrive at Bill's bout midnight and fill him in on the conversation with Horseshoe, also the tattoo viewing. I am not any closer to solving this crime than I am last week. I have bits and pieces of a story and there's a man who is lucky to be alive. I have money delivered by a mysterious man wearing glasses. I have a punk ass that won the race on a ringer but is so arrogant that he maintains his status on the track. I have a widowed sister who has to care for two teen-age boys. Yet, I still don't have a person to nab. I wrote the numbers down on a sheet of paper, 4589766.

I'm keyed up so I grab a brewski from the fridge and sit on the porch, drinking and smoking. This is what I do the best. I feel myself nodding off. I accidentally drop the bottle and burn my finger on the cigarette, shit, I need to go to sleep. I hear something.

"Do you want me to kiss the finger?" I turn around and face Mary. She has a nighty on that barely covers her ass, and she's standing in the doorway to my room. I guess she has been waiting for me. Lucky me. She walks over and straddles me on the rocker and plants a big kiss on me. I feel aroused. Mary could always arouse me. "We need to get to know each other again," she says. I nod, sort of paralyzed. She takes my hand and leads me to my bed. She carefully takes my clothes off. When she does, she spots the mummy wrap but she doesn't say a word. I wonder if she will make it feel any better than Gretchen did. When I am totally relaxed, she does her thing. The evening is wonderful. We talk about old times, laugh and cry. Ah yes, the scent of a woman. I have been lucky enough to smell it twice on this trip.

CHAPTER FOURTEEN

The morning is upon us quickly. We have a ton of work to do today. Bill has already left for the track. Mary and I are joining Ellie for breakfast and coffee when the phone rings, it's Bill. He wants to talk to me.

"We got some news. My early morning rover spots a guy wearing a horseshoe pinky ring. He gets a good look at him, it's Jack Whalen."

"Keep him in the barn area, I'll be there in thirty minutes." Mary overhears. "What's going on?"

"We have a lead on something, I got to go. Mary set up an appointment with the Wagering Facilitator to review the print-outs from that race. Have him explain how they work and how to read them. I'll be in touch later. Do not wander around until I have briefed you on what's going on up here. Is that clear?" She nods. I think she is figuring out the danger involved. I explained a little when we were in the sack last night. I zip out the door.

I'm glad we may have something, besides the fixed race, on Whalen and Freon. I had planned to talk to both of them anyway, so this is a perfect excuse to pull the noose a little tighter on Whalen. If he was in that valley he must be feeling guilty about something, otherwise he wouldn't have saved Jacob's life. I pull into the track and wave at the old codger who is manning the guard gate. I drive to the guard shack, Bill is waiting and pointing.

"Barn L, let's go." We drive the beater to barn L.

It is a typical morning in the barn area. There is hustling and bustling all over the place. I see Horseshoe putting new feet on a horse. He spots me, but doesn't acknowledge. I got him right where I want him. Bill spots Whalen, since I don't know what he looks like. We stop and get out.

"Hey, Whalen," Bill shouts. "Come here a minute boy." Whalen trots over. He is just a kid, apparently learning the business. I hope he doesn't learn the wrong things. This kid doesn't look like a hoodlum to me, but looks can be deceiving. "This is Sal Domino, he wants to ask you some questions. You don't have a problem with that do you Jack?" The boy shakes his head.

"Can we go where it is quieter?" I follow him to the tack room.

"What can I do for you Domino?" He seems like a pretty hard-nosed kid.

"I'm going to get to the point, Whalen. If I were you I wouldn't screw with me. I'm sure you already know who I am. Is that clear Jack?" I stare at him. I usually can tell if a man has balls when I stare.

He tilts his head, "I'll do the best I can, go ahead."

"How much did Butch Green offer you to box in Jacobs in the fixed race?" The question takes him by surprise.

"What you talkin' about? You gone crazy? I drive all my horses to win. I don't need to box anyone in," he plays the roll. I stare.

"Listen, punk. I told you I'm not screwin' around with you. You be straight with me or I'll have your ass in the clink for aiding and abetting a murder. Shall we try again, Whalen?"

"Now, wait a minute, Domino. I didn't kill anyone. I wasn't part of that. . .," he catches himself.

"Go ahead, Whalen. Let me hear something I can use. If I like it, I'll see if I can help you. If I don't like it, I'll hang your ass with the rest of them." Bill is standing outside the door. He peeks in to see if all is okay. I wave him off and wait for the kid to answer.

"I ain't gonna hang for that little, loud-mouthed asshole. That little prick is crazy. Listen, Domino, They paid me a good sum of money to strong-arm those favorites. Freon and I were riding shotgun to make sure Jacobs and Olmstead didn't get in on the money. But I ain't involved in no murder. No sir, you can't pin that on me!"

I persist, "How much were you paid?"

He pauses, "I ain't testifying against no one, you hear. I ain't gonna die like those other guys, no sir," he pleads. He's very nervous but continues, "How you gonna help me, those thugs will kill me if they find out I talk. You don't know these guys, Domino, there is a lot of money at stake here," he explains.

I do know these guys. They have beaten my ass a time or two. I'm still waiting for an answer.

"Twenty thousand. Twenty lousy, stinkin' thousand dollars to get involved in this shit. I ain't gonna die, Domino. You have to protect me," he pleads for about the fifth time.

"I told you I will do what I can. Now, we have another detail to discuss. Why were you out in that gully following Jacobs? If you were involved in the race, why did you want to be around Jacobs?" He looks stunned again.

"I heard you are good, Domino. Maybe you can get these guys after all. I ain't hangin' for these assholes. But, I'm not gonna testify either. I'll tell you what I know, then I'll get outa here. I'll fend for myself. I can hide and they will never find me. I got some cash that will keep me alive for awhile." He'd better be invisible.

"I'm listening."

"I knew for a couple of weeks they were gonna do something. They didn't tell us any details, just follow directions and don't ask any questions. I ain't dumb mister, so I follow orders. Green runs the show. He tells Freon and me what to do and who to look for on the track. We do as we are told. After the race, I get real jittery, and scram out of there. I didn't have a drive in the last race. As I am leaving the paddock, I see Jacobs runnin' so I follow him. He was there for a couple of days. This Caddy with some big hoods in it followed him, and they were just sitting in the car.

A few days later I see the Caddy at the tracks. They were talking with someone, so I follow them. They went to where Jacobs was hanging out. They jump his ass and throw him in the Caddy. I haven't been paid my money yet, but I think, maybe, I can hustle some more if I see what is goin' on. I follow them to a farm out in the country. I park way back so they don't see me. I walk to the barn and see them torture Jacobs. I wait too long because the wise guys come out and throw Jacobs in the trunk of the Caddy. Now, I've seen enough, but I still feel I can get some more cash if I see what is goin' on, so I follow them. They stop on this hill and get out of the Caddy. They grab Jacobs out of the trunk and throw his ass down this gully. They leave. I leave as well, but I feel like shit. I go and get my brother and we drive back to the site. We walk down the bank and find Jacobs still alive. Unbelievable; the man is still alive! I don't know where Jacobs lives, so I search him and find his wallet. The address is a place in Cyprus. We drive him to his truck. I lay him in the back of the truck, and drive, while my brother follows in my truck. We find the house okay and carry him to the front door. He is still alive. I ring the doorbell, then we haul ass. I figure I did my good deed for the day," he finishes.

"Good story, Whalen. Let me give you some advice. Get the hell out of here. Your story jives with what I know. You are in danger because you are part of the fix and they can kill you any time. You say you got the cash, then haul ass. Who paid you the money?"

"Some big hood wearin' shades. He didn't speak, just handed me an envelope. I wasn't gonna count it, he is a scary lookin' asshole. I've been layin' kinda low, so maybe I should lay lower by getting' outa here. Is that what you are sayin' Domino?" I nod.

"By the way, how did you know it was me that found

Jacobs, I'm just curious?" I point to the pinky ring.

"Damn. Domino, I'm gone. I don't train any horses, I just drive, so I'll get my tack and leave." That was the last time I saw that young man alive.

Bill sees Whalen fly out of the door. He sticks his head in and says, "What did you do to that little shit?" I smile and tell him I'll fill him in later. We drive back to the guard shack. It is late morning, so I suggest we grab a bite in the track kitchen. We enter, and the voices drop to a quiet murmur. We buy a BLT sandwich with some fries and a coke for a two bucks, the price can't be beat. I tell Bill the story. He agrees that Whalen is on the level, and also agrees with me to let him go. The kid is a dead man anyway, he just doesn't know when. They'll find his young ass and when they do there will be no body to be found. The kid will just vanish. I suppose I'll read about a missing person and know they got him. I need to talk to Freon. Bill tells me he has a large stable in barn Z, the last barn in the stable area.

After lunch I drive to barn Z, the place is quiet. It seems strange that there is no activity for such a large barn. I walk to barn Y, next to Z, and ask if they have seen Freon around. The groom tells me that all the workers left real early this morning and no one has been back since. The race office has been trying to reach him all morning on the intercom. I get in the Chevy and turn it around to point out. I loosen the strap in the thirty-eight's holster and walk to the barn. I look in the stalls and find them dirty. The horses do not look as if they have been fed and there is horseshit everywhere. According to Bill he has all twenty-four stalls in this barn, yet there is no one around. The obvious place to look is the tack room. I find the room and the door is ajar. I stand to the side, pull the thirty-eight out, and tap the door open. Freon is there but he will not be talking to anyone. He is hanging from the rafters with a noose around his neck, pulled very tight. I look closer and see he is not breathing. He is dead. I grab the cell phone and call the track. I ask for security. It rings and Bill answers, I tell him to get up to barn Z in a hurry.

Bill arrives in a jiffy and eyes the body. He says we have got to call the cops, I nod. Before he does, I look around. If this is a suicide, there has to be a message of some kind. I glance over the room and do not see anything special. On a desk is a manual of some kind. I open it and find the note.

I can't go on. I owe the bookies too much. The money from the race will not bail me out so I'll bail myself out. Screw everyone.

I show the note to Bill, "I guess he had a lot of problems."

"Sal, he was a private guy, a loner. He didn't have a family I can recall. He liked to buy horses at the auction, fix them up and race them. He was the owner, trainer and driver of all these horses. The overhead is low. I guess he bet on other things besides horses."

It's a shame that I didn't even get to meet the guy, what a tragedy. I ask Bill what will happen to the horses. Bill explains that the other trainers will send their grooms to tidy up the place, then the horses will go back to the auction or the killers. That's the way it is at a cheap track.

We wait for the police. When they arrive, the barn area is abuzz with rumors, one of them has me killing Freon, I love it. The police put their yellow tape around the whole barn, after the race department moved the horses to other locations. I don't know how they keep up with it all, they must have a system in place. There is no racing today, so Bill and I call it a day and go join the ladies. Before I do, I swing by Gretchen's barn to check on her. The place is immaculate, so I leave one of my cards under the tack room door. It's just a little some-thing to let her know I'm thinking of her and the kids.

I need a beer! Bill and I drive separately to his house. The ladies are preparing dinner. We grab some brews after saying hello. Bill has to hug Ellie, but I don't go near Mary, a nice lit-tle nod is sufficient. She knows my moods better than anyone does and she knows I'm in one of those moods now. I drink two brews and smoke two cigs. I blew it. I should have detained Whalen, I didn't figure Freon would check out on me the way he did. The Whalen boy will be dead soon. There is no way I can find him, unless I find him dead, in which case he is no damn good to me!

I sit through dinner like a zombie. I probably don't taste the London broil, boiled potatoes, cream corn and the brew. I'm sure it is good. I excuse myself and go to the porch to continue the smoking and drinking. Mary comes out to visit and I know what she is thinking. There he goes again, drinking and smoking. That is why we are not together now, because of my "habits." That is what she calls them. I like to call them characteristics. Well, shit, they are mine, whatever you want to call them! I want to be alone and Mary senses that. The night goes quickly when you down as many brews as I did. After awhile, I stumble to my apartment and pass out. Mary will not keep me company tonight, not this drunken guy.

CHAPTER FIFTEEN

I'm hurting this morning. I look a little sheepish when I see everyone, but they know me. I'll be fine. At breakfast, Mary and I discuss her conversation with the Wagering Facilitator with respect to the printouts. As they are going over the betting patterns, the judges call for a copy too. Well, better late than never. Mary explains to me there are too many national locations where bets were placed on Wildwood that afternoon. It will take forever to find the people who cashed the winning combination. I ask her to continue the investigation of the bets that were cashed on track. Perhaps we can find a pattern at this track. Of course, if a person is in on the scam, they sure as hell won't cash the ticket on track and risk being identified. Meanwhile, the lady that attacked the General Manager, Gil Holden, has filed a lawsuit against the track and the state citing incompetence. Her suit alleges that the track and state lost institutional control and she is suing for $5,000,000. It takes all kinds.

Mary has another appointment today with the Wagering Facilitator. She tells me he is very qualified, but suggests that the hoods pulled one over on everyone. It is a long shot, but maybe someone will surface who knew of the race beforehand, other than the participants.

As usual, Bill has already left for the track. I need to drive around and chill a bit. I think better when I'm on my own. I decide to drive to the inn, where I stayed before I was chased out for my own good. The place appears to be serene. The grounds are immaculate and overnight guests are beginning to check out to continue on their journeys. It looks like a peaceful inn at the foot of the Cascades, just as it is supposed to be.

I never turned my key in, so I parked in front of my old room, 21, I listened and waited. I didn't hear anything, so I ease to the door and try the key, it works. The room still smells like smoke and beer but it is very clean. I glance around but don't see anything. As I leave the room, I feel the doorjamb, the tape is still there. Apparently the wise guys didn't pick up on the trick. I was just too damn slow in combating them. I decide to go to the office and snoop around.

The little old lady at the desk looks up when I approach.

"Well hello, sonny. You left in a hurry the other day. I can refund you some money because you didn't stay all the days you paid for. I see you had car trouble too."

"Yes, ma'am. I did leave in a hurry. I was called out of this area on an emergency. Did you happen to pack the clothes I left behind?"

"Well, no. I didn't find any clothes," she coos.

Bill and I left all my stuff there. It is apparent that the hoodlums didn't expect me back either. I thank her and turn to go when I smell it, it is the same smell. That cheap perfume, it's the same scent I smelled during my two attacks. I'll bet it is the same odor that Jacobs smelled when they were breaking his ankle. I have to find out. I reach in to look at the registration book, so I can get closer to the old lady. The smell is coming from her. It is the same smell, I'm sure of it. She catches me looking.

"Can I help you find something sonny?"

"I am looking for the date when I registered. I can get a refund from my company. Sorry I intruded." She looks right through me. A hateful glint passed by her face for a split second, then she smiles.

"Here it is, check it yourself." I lean over to be sure and get another smell. I get a good whiff of the odor again and am certain it is the same smell. I look up and she is looking right through me again. I get a chill. I have to leave. I turn around and she is still looking at me. There is something wrong with this place, something dreadfully wrong. I think she may be the key to this case. I drive away hoping never to see that place again. Why would a little old lady be in the room when someone is beating my ass to a pulp, not once, but twice? If it were the same smell, why would a little old lady be present when some hoods are torturing a person to death? What kind of twisted mind would want to do that. I decide to have Bill check her out using the local cops. If I have to see that lady again, I want to be armed with more than my thirty-eight.

I drive to the track and hope to find Bill. As I approach the gate guard, the old-timer holds me up. He tells me that Bill had to go to the coroner's office about the suicide yesterday and for me to wait for him at the shack. I decide to visit Gretchen while I wait for Bill. I spot her washing a horse, I know she's busting her ass to keep up. They don't have a lot of horses, but the work is hard no matter how many you have. I want to talk to her.

"Hello, Gretchen." She turns around and smiles.

"Sal, how nice of you to come around. I found your card when I arrived this morning. Do you have any news on the murders yet?" The smile turns to a frown when she thinks of her brother's death.

" It's been a slow process, Gretchen. I feel that I have made progress, but I don't have all of the answers yet. I'm frustrated. Every time I take a step forward, it seems I get pushed back. Did you hear about Freon?"

"Yes, the barn area is full of rumors. Freon wasn't well liked, but no one wants to see anyone die. I hear he didn't have any family, is that right?" I nod. "What are they going to do with the horses?"

"Bill seems to think they will go to auction or go to the killers." That distresses her.

"I would like to buy some of the horses, I'm familiar with them. He did a good job with sore horses. He was a kind man, but not too sociable." I want to tell her to use the money.

"Gretchen, what did you do with the money?"

"I haven't touched it, Sal. I think it is dirty money, just like Paul describes in his letter." She breaks down. I don't dare touch her with all these people around.

"Gretchen, Paul said to use it for anything you want. Who cares if the money is dirty, the government will never find out, that's for sure," I plead. She weighs the idea.

"Oliver, the oldest boy, wants to learn how to drive. He wants to go into the business his dad was in. He's not much for school, so I think I'll allow him to do it. He can get his "A" license here at Wildwood. He's going to graduate from high school next month."

"Great, that's a wonderful idea. I love it!" A smile comes across her face. It will be hard for us to get together while Mary is in town. It is conceivable that we may never see each other again.

"Why don't you check with the race department and find out the status of the horses. If you can, buy some and increase the size of your stable," I reason. She likes the idea. I wave to her as I climb in the Chevy. She's beautiful, tough and smart, she'll get through this. When I get back to the guard shack, Bill is there. I fill him in on the episode at the inn and the weird vibes I got from that old lady. He says he will check her out. It's time for lunch and a visit to our favorite track kitchen. This time when we walk in, several horsemen walk out. It seems there is an attitude developing here. If a groom wasn't sleeping on a table, we would be the only people here. We order lunch from an unfriendly guy. We buy a hamburger, chips and a coke for $1.50. I walk back to the table by the window where we always sit and eat lunch. Now, I'm pissed. I've had it with these flunkies. I walk up to the caterer and get in his face.

"What the hell is the problem around here?" I yell at him.

"You wanna know, mister, I'll tell ya', these people are sick and tired of all the ridicule they are getting in the papers and from the town's people. Most of these horsemen work their ass off for peanuts, and they get shit on. They want you to solve this case, and do it fast, so they can carry on with their lives. That's the problem, mister, that's where I'm coming from," and he walks away. I deserve that. I have made some bad decisions in this case. These people are right, I need to get this thing settled, post haste. I can't eat my burger. I leave the kitchen and walk to the Chevy. Bill follows me.

"Bill, let's get some info on that witch at the inn. I have a bad feeling about this lady." He gets right on it. As I am about to climb in the Chevy, Bill signals me to come in the office. The gate guard calls him to come right over. We walk together to the gate. The old- timer is a little white in the face. He gives Bill an envelope. Bill and I look at each other. Well, it can't be a bomb, it's too small. Bill opens the envelope and staring at us is one pinky finger with a horseshoe ring on it. No telling where the rest of the body is. Whalen didn't even make it out of town!

I'm shaken. Bill is calling the cops and will get the dope on that lady from the inn. I want to see Mary, so I go to the Wagering Facilitator's office. I find both of them checking the printouts from the race. I enter and Mary introduces me to Steve Effing, the Wagering Facilitator at Wildwood. I shake his hand and sit down for a lesson in gambling. For the next two hours he explains the process of wagering and cashing of winning tickets. He describes a national network where several thousand combinations are bet on all of the numbers, except the favorites. Of course, the legitimate bettors all use the favorites, as a bettor should. Bret told me that Paul's horse and his horse should have been the favorites in that race. He explains that if the race were legit the numbers that came in, based on the horses past performance lines, should pay several hundred thousand dollars. Instead, because those favorites are eliminated from the wise guy bets, the payoff is significantly lower. Much lower than expected. He reasons that several thousand tickets are bet leaving the favorites out. That is called a score. The race fixers don't care what the price is, because they have several thousand tickets on the winning combination. When you can eliminate the favorites the odds of fixing a race are better. There was a similar setup at a thoroughbred track in Florida some years ago. The practice is not uncommon in pari-mutuels, but it usually is not this obvious. Very few people know about a fixed race, that is why they are successful and the culprits rarely come to justice. Because the price is so small, the outstanding winning tickets number in the thousands, all over the country. He says that whoever put this race together has an extensive network on a national scale. Mr. Effing has been very helpful but he doesn't know about the ringer.

We thank him and leave the office. I tell Mary that I have to talk with Bill and I'll meet her at the house. I hope Bill has found some information on that old lady, she gives me the creeps. We drive our separate ways. I see the beater and pull in. He has the info.

"Her name is Glenda Jackson. Sal, she looks like a sweet old lady, but she's a two-time loser, extortion on one, and assault with a deadly weapon on the second. She did time on both counts. Her husband's family owned the inn for several years, then willed it to him. He died mysteriously last year, and she took over the inn," he explains. My eyes lit up. This old bitch is behind the sting, I know it. I still don't know why they have kept me alive. Do they think they can buy me?

"Bill, I wonder if there is a connection to Butch Green? Can we pull his records and look at his background?" He gets the records.

"Look at this Sal." I look at the paper in front of me. It says that Butch Green is born to a Glenda Green.

"What are you getting at, Bill?" He gives me the police report about Glenda Jackson. Her maiden name is Green. Jesus, the little prick may be her son!

"Shit, Bill, good job. How in the hell can we tie them together to the crimes? The race fixing is one thing, but the murders are entirely different."

I'll bet that old bitch knocked off her husband too, mysterious illness, my ass. That woman is dangerous. I'll bet the old coot never knew what hit him. They have made a ton of money on this race and I'm sure that she has an account to which the money is being wired. I hope it is local.

We now have some leads and additional information, but nothing to go to the DA with. All we have is two more dead bodies, one of which will never be found. I need a beer now. The drive to Bill's house is a short one, but when the mind is cluttered, it's tougher. Dinner is being prepared as we enter the driveway. I wash up and join the table. Mary recognizes that mood again and leaves me alone. I have to come up with something, anything to rattle their cage. The baked eggplant with sauce and antipasto is delicious, right out of my mom's cookbook. I am mentally exhausted. These people are grinding on me. I excuse myself, and light up on the porch. I will not have a drink, I need to think. The night passes with my mind still racing three thousand miles an hour. I keep going back to those numbers on that horse's lip. There has to be a connection, somewhere. I go to sleep, alone again, thinking about those damn numbers.

CHAPTER SIXTEEN

It's Sunday morning when I wake up. It feels good to wake up without a hangover, maybe I'll try it again sometime. The track will be racing this afternoon and I decide to lay low for a while. I feel I don't need to be seen today, based on what that cook told me yesterday. Bill can fill me in on any news he may find. I feel like visiting Gretchen, but I know she is racing a couple of horses today, and she'll be busy tending, maybe tomorrow. I feel for the cell phone, it needs to be charged. I use Bill's phone to call Susan Lockhart to check on Bret Jacobs.

"Hello, Lockhart residence, Jacob speaking," says the polite little guy.

"Jacob, this is Mr. Domino, the man you met the other day who is helping your uncle," I explain. He catches on.

"Yes, I remember. Do you want to talk to my mom?"

"Yes, I do, thanks. Is she busy?"

"She is washing Uncle Bret, I'll get her, just hold on," he says.

Before I could stop him, he is off like a flash. Tough kid to hold down.

Susan answers, "hello, Sal, it is nice of you to call."

"How is Bret today? I hope he is doing fairly well."

"He's hanging in there. Are you coming up for a visit?"

"I would like too, will that be a problem? I don't want to break in on anything you have planned."

"We would love to have you. Please come. When can I expect you? I will prepare a little something to eat."

"Allow me to run some errands. I'll be there in two hours."

"Terrific, I'll inform Bret you are on you way. He admires

you greatly, Sal. He likes your determination in this case." I'm the one who is respectful of Bret, it is a miracle he's alive. I will tell him about Whalen.

The Chevy needs to be gassed and I need cigs, so the usual stop is made to fill both orders. I didn't let anyone know where I'm going. I need to be alone and think. It may be that Bret can tell me something about Whalen that will allow me to look in another direction. Also, I will have to tell him about Freon's suicide. I will not drive by the Venticello, don't want more negative thoughts to clutter my brain. Instead, I'll take a third route past the Castle Pines Resort, another one of our stomping grounds. The place looks fantastic as I approach the property. It is no longer the Castle Pines, it is now a retirement community called the Woodland Estates. The new owners have taken great care in preserving the grounds. At least one of our hangouts ia alive and well. The Castle Pines is where we used to go skinny-dipping all the time. It was a Jewish resort and the little Jewish girls liked to play in the water after dark. All the guys jumped in with them, we never fooled around, just had fun. We got to know each other pretty well in those days. We always talked about what we would do when we went back to the city for school. It was just good fun. Kids these days have to smoke dope and gang bang to get their rocks off. We respected each other, no matter what our background was. I think we had a better handle on things than our parents did. The parents were still hung up on all the prejudice bullshit.

Cyprus is upon me in a flash. Time always flies for me when I reminisce about my childhood. I find the house, drive to the supermarket lot and turn around. I drive back down the street and park pointing in the right direction. I walk to the back door and knock. Susan opens the door for me.

"Bret is taking a nap, come in to the kitchen and have a sandwich," she offers. I nod and follow her. The table is already set.

"This bread is baked fresh this morning. Sunday is a busy time for the deli. People come out of church and want items for lunch. I asked for the day off because Bret had a rough night. I think he was dreaming," she explains.

"Will he be strong enough to talk to me today?"

"Yes, he is itching to talk. Jacob keeps him busy with some of his games, bless his heart. He wants Bret to get well fast, so he can watch him play football. How are you coming with the case? Can Bret help you anymore?"

"I have some news for him. I think Bret can give me some more ammo to combat these guys. His recollection has been remarkable. I'll sit on the porch and smoke until you come and get me." I thank her for the sandwich and head to the porch.

It doesn't take long. Susan informs me that Bret is alert and wants to talk. I put out the smoke and hoof it up the stairs. When I look at him this time, his face has some color in it and his skin is healing. I feel better about that. I know he is going to make it.

"How is the ankle?"

"Not bad. I have a problem when I get up, but the crutches help. I can go to the bathroom by myself now, I feel like a man again. My head is still groggy and the shoulders hurt but not that bad. Susan changes the leg wrap once in a while. I know the ankle will have to be set at a later date. Do you have any news to share?"

"Yes, I do. Freon hung himself in the tack room. The note he left says he owed a bookie too much and the fixed race didn't bail him out, so he bailed himself out," I explain. Jacobs hangs his head.

"Bill wasn't a friendly guy, but he sure knew how to put a sore horse together to race. He was the master of that. I'm sorry to hear of the suicide. The barn area knew that Bill gambled on football, really heavy at times. The news doesn't surprise me. He was always in the trap with those bookies. The interest they charged is astronomical. Even when he won, it was never enough to get out of the hole, the interest just kept piling up. When I heard that he was involved I knew he did it for the money. Freon was too good a horseman to cheat. The bookies got him in the end," he explains. This is a case where a good guy gets swallowed up, the bookies and the race fixers.

"I also had a long talk with Whalen. He's a cocky little shit. I got a lot from him. He was the one who found you Bret. He and his brother saved your ass." He takes a huge breath. I tell him the story about Whalen tailing him, and watching the horror. I also told him that Whalen didn't care about his safety, but wanted more money from these guys. He figured he could get some. His conscience got to him and he returned to the scene and dragged you up the slope and drove you to Susan's. I informed him that I told Whalen to get out of town ASAP. I told him that Whalen didn't move fast enough and the pinky finger with the ring attached was a reminder of their power.

Paul rubs his chin; "so it was Whalen's finger I saw that night?" I nod. "Tough break for the kid. He thought he could run and hide from these monsters, fat chance. I assume he is dead?" I don't move. He can figure it out.

"Bret, can you tell me more about Butch Green?"

"I've been racking my brain about that little weasel. I know he's got the muscle behind him, but I don't know where to look for it."

"Do you know anything about the inn at the Cascades, south of town?" His hand brushes his hair.

"No, not really, why do you ask?"

"I think there is a connection between Green and the owners there. I've been snooping around and I get bad vibes from the place. Besides, I was jumped twice when I was staying there. Do you remember about the smell the night of your attack? Do you remember telling me about a smell, maybe a fag smell from the city? Can you remember that part of the conversation?" He is thinking. I wait.

He blurts out, "I remember; I said it smelled like a woman

but it is men that are beating my ass to a pulp, but I did smell a woman's perfume. I'm sure of that now," he states. I need him to smell that stuff to confirm it. I have a plan that will include Mary, she'll love it. We talked casually, then I could see he was getting sleepy, so I let him doze off and I eased down the stairs, quietly. I see Susan in the kitchen.

"That's enough for today. I'll be in touch." Not so fast, Domino. She swings in front and blocks me, giving me that look again. I don't think I can handle this.

"What's your hurry, Sal. Jacob's playing football and Bret is sleeping. We can have some quality time together," she coos.

"You are quite lovely and I know you are lonely, but the timing isn't right for us now, maybe at a later date when all this stuff is behind us." She lets go of me. I head for the door.

I pacify her by saying,"you are doing a great job with Bret." She nods, and walks away.

Not too many men would give up a piece of ass on a wonderful Sunday morning, but I'm not into it right now. My system is all screwed up. Lovemaking is the farthest thing from my mind. I have to return to Bill's and work out a plan to trick that little weasel Green.

As I'm driving back to Bill's house I get an idea. These people don't know Mary, at least I don't think they do, so I'm going to dispatch her to the inn to converse with the little old lady. She can act as if she is lost, and looking for directions, or something like that. When she engages her in conversation, she can smell the perfume. Mary can make small talk and ask what kind it is. If she finds out what kind it is, I'll buy it and run up to Cyprus and allow Bret to smell it. Can it be that simple?

I'm also thinking about the weasel. Usually when an owner, trainer, driver like Green, has so many horses, he needs a layover spot. I'm guessing he has a farm some place where he freshens up horses when they need a break. If I find the

farm I'll find some proof. These two thoughts bring me to
Bedford. I drive to Bill's house and pull around to the apartment. To my surprise, Mary is in the apartment cleaning.
Mercy, I have been beset with some fine ladies on this case.
Mary has always thought of me as a slob, so I appreciate the
job. Maybe she wants to bunk in with me, and wants the place
to be tidy. Nah, I screwed that up the past two nights because
of my moods. I don't think she can take the inconsistency. I
don't want to surprise her by changing now.

"Hello Mary. What are you doing?' She turns to me and
smiles.

"You know how neat I like things to be. I thought you
could use the help, knowing how busy you are on this case. I
just wish I could do more for you." Boy, did I time this right.

"Mary, you have hit the jackpot. I need you to do something for me. Are you up to playing a charade on someone?"
Her eyes light up.

"Shit yes, Sal. I'll do anything to get you back to normal."

I tell her the plan, and she loves it. She'll go this afternoon
and guarantees she will get the info we need. She's excited,
until I tell her what I suspect about the little old lady. I warn
her that she could be dangerous and to watch her pretty ass. I
drive to the track and find Bill. He is in the paddock, but the
rover finds him for me. We need to talk. The rover drops him
off and we walk to the beater. We climb in and head for the
little café on the outskirts of town where we had lunch once
before. We order sandwiches and cokes.

"Bill, do you know if Butch Green has a farm in the area?"

"Not offhand, Sal. Why?"

"With the size of his stable, I figure he has to have a lay
up farm to freshen horses. If we can locate the farm, if there is
one, maybe we can get some facts. It's worth a shot." Bill
agrees and will work on it. I also ask him if Butch has any
brothers or cousins he knows about. He nods at that one too. I
tell him I'm going to cruise to the paddock and wait until he

calls.

The pass Bill gives me allows access to the paddock. I enter with my Mets hat on and slide around. I'm not noticed, thank goodness. I walk to a stall where Butch is tacking a horse for a race. He doesn't see me, so I can observe him closely. The little shit really is a good horseman, why does he have to fix races? Maybe the old witch has him over a barrel. I'm going to find out soon, I have a feeling. Bill calls the cell phone and wants to meet at the guard shack. I hustle out. Bill is waiting for me when I arrive and he's smiling.

"Bingo! There is a farm and it's not too far from here. One of my contacts owes me a favor and came up with it. He over-heard some people talking in the paddock, apparently this place is hush, hush. The contact says they already brought Jumpin' Jimmy there. They got the registration papers from the race office and shipped him out, I confirmed it with my guard at the gate. Can you guess who the contact is?"

"Is it Horseshoe?" He nods.

"Horseshoe says to be sure and tell the copper what he did for us. He wants to know if we are going to rip those drug papers up." We look at each other and start roaring, fat chance! 'shoe!

CHAPTER SEVENTEEN

Bill finds the directions to the farm. The drive will take about thirty minutes and I need a plan. Bill did not indicate to me that Green has any relatives, so basically, I'll sneak to the farm without any knowledge of anything or anyone. I don't like that, because the odds are not in my favor. I have learned from past dealings, odds need to be on your side. The Chevy is raring to go. There is only one way to the village of Drawbridge, and I take it. The only entrance into the village is a drawbridge, hence the name. I don't like that either because the habit of backing in or pointing in the right direction will have no bearing here if I can't get out. I don't like this at all. I arrive at the rickety old drawbridge, it has seen better days. I wonder how it holds a trailer full of horses? I guess it's stronger than it looks. The road is narrow. The foliage is pretty to watch, but I don't give a shit about Mother Nature at the present time, I need to find evidence. It is slow going but I am patient. The road widens a bit and I spot a small farm on my right. There are three large pastures surrounding the main building. I count seven horses in the pastures, not one of them is Jimmy. For what it's worth, I make a U-turn and point the Chevy in the get-away position. I park behind a large oak on the apron of the road, get out, lock the door and check the thirty-eight. I crouch and sneak my way to the barn. I can't hear voices, but someone has to look after this place. As I continue on, I notice a mobile home to the left of the barn, it can't be seen from the road. I hear horses neighing, I work my way to the barn and hide in some bushes. An open window is close by, I sneak a look. The window is positioned to look right down the aisle. There are several stalls on each side. The place is much bigger than it looks from the road. The aisle is raked to perfection. The stall work must be completed at this time of day and the horses turned out to pasture. The work seems easy but fixing a race isn't. There isn't a door close to the window where I'm standing, which means I have to move to either side to gain entrance. That also means I will be exposed. As I slip from the window position and walk to the north end of the barn, I hear noises. I stop. Music is coming from the mobile home. I walk down the aisle, looking inside each stall. I reach the south end and the last stall reveals what I'm looking for.

Jimmy is lying at an angle, and he doesn't appear to be moving. I don't know how to check a pulse on a dead horse, so I walk past the chain and feel his neck. He's cold and dead, very dead. Rigor mortis is setting in. I have a dead ringer in front of me. I am still bothered by the numbers under his lip; so I crouch down in the straw and turn his head towards me. This isn't the most pleasant thing I have done in recent memory, so I suck it up and get real close to his mouth to read those damn numbers. I pull the lip up and read 4589766, exactly as they should read. When I move to put the horse's head down, something catches my eye. I look again at what I see. It seems from this angle that the eight has a different shade to it. I look again from a different angle, and sure enough the shade is different. That's not an eight, it's a three. The three has been altered to look like an eight! I review the rest of the numbers and see the seven has a different shade to it also. Of course, a one has been altered to look like a seven. If I'm correct, the numbers should now read 4539166, not 4589766. Can this be possible? How can all the officials miss this? I memorize the numbers and prepare to leave. As I look down the aisle, I have left a neat trail of footsteps. Inside a stall close to where I'm standing is a rake. I use the rake to cover my trail as I walk backwards to the north end of the barn. When I finish, it passes inspection. The only problem is that I have to leave the rake on the opposite end of the barn from where I borrowed it. I hope no one notices. Do I dare check the mobile home? I would like to find out who the caretaker is. Whoever it is killed the fake Jimmy. I reach for the thirty-eight and grip it tightly in my right hand. I run to the nearest side of the mobile home and peek in a window, and washing dishes is a big guy wearing shades. He resembles the guy who delivered the monies, roughed me and Bret up, and committed the murders. He still has to work for someone. I walk quietly to the other end of the mobile home. Behind it is parked a Caddy, the same one that was seen before. The guy is definitely a hood, a strong-arm guy who takes care of the physical stuff for the race fixers. I have seen enough and get ready to sneak back to the Chevy. I hear a car coming, and I have to wait. Whoever it is will see the Chevy. I hope it isn't anyone that is involved with the case. I look up and see the truck stop at the beginning of the property. I notice a gate when I drive by earlier, but it is locked. The driver gets out, unlocks the gate and drives to the barn. I didn't see who it is. I'm safe because they didn't see the Chevy. I'm very lucky. My luck runs out when I see who the passengers are. The little old lady, Glenda Jackson, opens the driver door and circles to the passenger door. She opens the door and drags a person out of the seat, it's Mary. She is blind-folded and gagged, and her hands appear to be tied. Shit, I didn't need this to happen. I underestimated the old bitch. Bill tried to warn me but I think I am smarter than she is. I can't leave now, I've got to get Mary out of here. They will torture her just like they did to those other people, then possibly kill her, or leave her for dead.

I guess Mary wasn't convincing enough when she asked about the perfume. The old lady must have seen through that charade in a heartbeat. How stupid of me to allow her to be put in danger. I'm sure they don't know I'm here, so I sneak back to the window and peek in. I hear voices.

"Bruno, I have a little present for you," the old lady

shouts. I hear the mobile home door open and a trudging of steps to the barn. Bruno appears in the doorway, taking up all the space.

"My, mom, she is a pretty thing, thanks." Mom, oh God, she produced another asshole like Butch, except this man is huge.

"I don't want you to touch her Bruno until we have finished with her. Do you understand Bruno?" He nods, like a little boy. "This lady is very important to us. We will use her as bait to draw out that Domino asshole. I think he'll back off once he finds out his honey is here with me. After we are done with her and leave, I don't care what you do with her, just get rid of the body in the lake, like you did with that Whalen jerk. How did Domino think he could get away with a stupid trick like the perfume thing? It is my fault that I wear it," she reasons. They put Mary in a tack room, shut the door and go to the mobile home. I wait until I hear their voices inside the mobile home and then beat a path to the tack room. The hell with the footprints. I touch the handle, and it swings loose. I look in and she's tied to a chair. I walk in, take the gag out of her mouth, and clasp my hand over her mouth, I tell her it is me. When I remove the blindfold, tears start running down her face and she gives me a big hug. I hold my finger to my lips, she understands. I untie her and we prepare to leave. I whisper 'follow me' and we run to the north end away from the mobile home. I dash to the Chevy, with Mary close behind. I unlock the door, push her in the driver's side, follow her in, start the car and ease away, quietly. I remember the bridge. I hope no is guarding it, because their ass will be run over. I drive over the bridge, slowly and proceed to Bill's house. I look over at Mary and she is crying uncontrollably. I let her go as I hustle to safety. I try not to speed, but I can't help it. If I get pulled over, I'll show some ID and bullshit my way out of it. We reach Bill's in twenty minutes. I pull around to the back of the apartment and this time I turn around to face in the direction looking out. We haven't said a word. I open my door and rush around to her side. I ease her out and carry her to my room. I find the bed quickly and set her down. Ellie sees me pull in and meets me in the room. She gasps as She sees Mary sprawled on the bed.

"What happened, Sal? Is she alright?" I nod

"Phone Bill at the track for me Ellie, and tell him to get here ASAP." I tend to Mary. She's still shaking with fear.

"Mary, let me know when you want to talk about it, okay?" She nods.

A few moments pass. In the meantime I swig a brewski and smoke a cig. We are not in any hurry. I prefer she wait for Bill anyway, because I don't want her to tell the story twice. I hear the beater, it's hard not to hear the beater. The car door opens and shuts quickly. Bill arrives at the door and looks in. He is, as I am, braced for the story she's ready to tell.

"I guess the trick didn't work, huh Sal?" She smiles at me. I'm so glad to see her smile, I almost grab and hug her. She continues.

"I drive to the inn just as we discussed. I get out, walk to the office and wait a second for a clerk. This nice, sweet look-ing old lady comes to greet me. How cute she is. I ask her the fastest way to the city from the mountains. She describes it and I take notes to make it look easy. I pretend to smell some-thing. She asks, what's wrong. I tell her I like the perfume and ask her the name of it. Her face goes stone cold. A smile quickly replaces the frown. I should have realized something right there. She told me the name of the perfume and I write it down. She continues with the directions. When we are fin-ished, she asks me if I want to see her perfume collection, she has them from all over the world. I say sure, and follow her into the back room--bad move on my part. She points to a desk with lots of bottles on it. I walk to the desk and that is the last thing I remember. I think she slugs me with something and then the next thing I know is that I'm tied, blindfolded and gagged then put in the front seat of a truck and made to lay down. I'm in and out of consciousness, but I do not recall her saying anything. I know we are alone. I'm thinking to myself, what are they going to do with me. You didn't tell me any details, so I didn't know what to expect. You just warned me about the lady, but she looks so sweet, I couldn......," She breaks down again. We leave her alone for a while. Ellie is there to comfort her until she is ready to speak again.

"When we approach a stop, she tells me about the man I'll meet. This man likes to play with nice ladies like you. I begin to cry through the blindfold and she tells me to stop the whining. I am pulled out of the truck and dragged inside. You know the rest. How did you find me, Sal?"

It was pure luck that I was at the farm the same time that they brought Mary back.

"I was following a lead that Bill got for me. They brought you to a farm that is owned by Butch Green and his mother. The lady that kidnapped you is Green's mother and that other 'git must be her son from another marriage. That is a frightening thought. I happened to be there, snooping around and heard a car coming. When I saw you being dragged from the car I figured out that the woman had caught on. By the way, I found Jumpin' Jimmy dead in a stall. Bill, you know how I fuss over those damn tattoos, well, when I looked at the numbers under the top lip, I catch a glimpse of a shade difference. After I mess with his mouth I realized that the three had been changed to an eight and the one had been changed to a seven. I'll bet any amount of money that the dead horse is a quality animal that fit the bill for the switch. They don't come across too many of these situations, but this was a chance to switch a horse and fool everyone. The number should read 4539166, instead it read 4589766. If we look up that number, we'll find the dead horse's name and the name of the ringer. Now we have to concentrate on nabbing the old lady, and her two sons," I explain.

Everyone looks stunned. It is late and Ellie fixes a nice a tray of sandwiches, but no one is hungry. I take Mary to the room and wait for her outside while she showers and dresses for bed. The bathroom light goes off and I slip into the room. She is in bed and I cuddle her up with some extra pillows and a blanket. She looks peaceful and whispers 'thank you' with her eyes closed. I take a shower and join her in bed. We don't fool around tonight. We have other things on our mind, like catching this ruthless family. I would like to be a fly on the wall when they find out Mary is missing.

CHAPTER EIGHTEEN

The morning comes quickly. Mary screams a few times in the night, a nightmare, but I won't tell her. It's Monday and the track will be busy as usual, talking about the races from the weekend and all the scuttlebutt about which horse will bring home the trophy in this year's stake race. I don't recall seeing any horse that looks special this weekend. I check the results and Gretchen's horses win two races. I will have to stop by and congratulate her. Butch raced thirteen horses this weekend but wins only once. Maybe he has a lot on his mind, like me. I want to stay on that little turkey as much as I can. I plan on visiting the race Secretary today to see if he can find in a database the tattoo number of the deceased horse. I'm also certain the real Jumpin' Jimmy is dead. I have to get some hard evidence that will convict these people, plus find the leak from my department. It also is apparent I will not have to visit Bret Jacobs again, since I know were it was coming from.

I now have to concentrate on Butch's farm and watch him here at the track. He will slip up, and I'll be there to grab him. It is possible that the little old lady has spoken to her son this morning about last night's events. I ask Mary to stay with Ellie for the day, she doesn't need to be seen around town. I drive to the track to find Bill. I inform him I'm going to rattle that little shit's chain and does he want to be there. I drive to barn X to talk to Butch Green. I do not park at the top of the hill, but on the bottom near Horseshoe's blacksmith shop. I feel safer there because I still got old 'shoe on a string. I walk to the barn with Bill at the bottom of the hill. I hear that pesky little voice from my car. The voice gets louder as I reach the barn, "finish those stalls by noon or I'll fire your ass", I hear, what a nice guy. As I approach him he stumbles a bit and yells, "What do you want Domino? I don't have times for your silly ass games this morning, I have to ship some horses to race in Pennsylvania," he shouts.

"Good morning to you too, Butch. What a wonderful morning it is. You should have a nice trip shipping those horses from your farm, yes, indeed, a real comfortable trip." I stare right at his punk ass, and wait for a reaction, it comes suddenly.

"Domino, I don't have a farm. Do you think I can afford a farm off the winnings this track pays, no way, Jose!" He laughs.

"Gee, that's not what your Mom tells me, she says you make a pile of money at this track. I was out there yesterday Butch, a real nice spread. Must cost a ton of money to keep it up though. Do you spend as much time there as your Mother and Bruno do?" I want to set him off. He sees where I am going and doesn't take the bait.

"Domino, you must use both hands when you jack off, because you are getting senile. I don't know what the hell you are talking about."

"Play it your way, Butch. I'll catch up to you sooner than later, you and your conniving two time loser of a mother and that big oaf you got for a brother." Boy, I know how to set a guy off. With that last remark, he charges me, this time he's sober. He leaps on top of me and we wrestle to the ground. He is a strong son-of-a-bitch. The force of his leap rolls us down the hill into a drainage ditch. I get lucky and land on top of the little shit. I chop him in the jaw swiftly, and only once. Gosh, this guy can't take a punch. Bill is there by my side, but is not needed. No one comes to the aid of Green. I accomplish what I set out to do, and that is to rattle his chain. While I begin to walk away, he gets up and fixes his soggy clothes.

"You shouldn't talk about people's mommas, Domino. That's not a nice thing to say. My mom is a nice, sweet lady, and you will pay for those remarks, I promise."

"Are you threatening a law enforcement officer, Green?"

His glare can kill one of those horses he drives. "It's a promise, Domino, a dead-ass promise." He walks backwards up the hill, not taking his eyes off me.

"Damn, Sal, I heard that some of the tactics you use in the field won't make any handbooks, but that is really nasty, " observes Bill.

"He's a scumbag, Bill. He's just like a snake that lives under these rocks we are standing on. He gives every good, honest horseman a bad name, and I'm going to nail his ass. You can take that to the bank," I stomp away.

I want to freshen up but I have that damn number on my mind, so I walk to the Race secretary's office, barge in and close the door. The actions and my looks take the old gent by surprise. I apologize and get right to the point.

"Sam, if I give you a tattoo number, can you look in some sort of database and find the horse's name?" He nods, apprehensively. "Good, take this number down, 4539166. Find it please, I'll wait." Bill is with me as Sam punches in the numbers. He's nervous over the keys and makes some mistakes in entering the info. He pauses. A strange look appears on his face.

"What's the matter, Sam?" I wait to see if the expression vanishes, it doesn't.

"I can't explain this, Mr. Domino. The info that appears with the identification numbers you submitted to me describes a stakes horse from California. It says that the horse has been retired for two years and that the last race line showing is August, 1997. Are you sure these numbers are correct?"

Without giving him any privileged info, I say, "I'm pretty sure they are correct, Sam. Why did you ask that question?"

"Usually the papers of a retired horse are turned in to national headquarters in Kansas City. That officially tells the racing world that this horse is no longer eligible or competi-

155

tive to race any longer."

I ask, "When you look at papers when a horse enters a race, how careful are you in looking at his ID numbers?"

"Well, we scan to be sure the number is correct. I'm more interested in the race lines to be sure he is entered in a competitive race to protect the wagering public," he explains.

"Can the numbers on the papers be altered?"

"I suppose they can but the tattoo can't be altered, so there is no benefit in faking the paper numbers," he explains further.

"Before you print a copy for me, interpret the race lines, then explain what a stakes horse is."

"Certainly. This horse is capable of racing in the very best company on a national scale. His breeding and race lines indicate he has won those types of races in the past. As he was in the midst of his career he became injured and was retired. It says here that he has a bowed tendon. The injury is not that serious, but he can't race against the same type of horses he has in the past. He will not be as fast, but can compete at a lower level and still win."

"How low?"

"Oh, maybe high claiming; around $25,000 -30,000."

"Certainly, not $2,000, right?"

"Goodness gracious no, Mr. Domino. He would blow the field away." Sam's eyes light up, and he stares at me.

"You can print that copy now." He nods. "Thank you Sam, you are an experienced horseman. Bear in mind that several people have died because of these assholes and I don't want you to be one of them. Do I make myself clear?" he nods again. He prints the info and gives it to me as his hands continue to shake. I give him a cold stare and walk out of the office with Bill behind me.

"Damn, Domino, you scared the shit out of that guy."

"I intended to, Bill. I want him to live."

We part company. I look at the copy that Sam furnished me. The name of the horse is Royal Brigade. He is, or was, a

156

killer on the track. He has won twelve races with winnings of approximately $200,000. He has raced and won nationwide. It's a shame he had to be retired because of an injury. Instead, his tattoos had been altered to read a different horse, and voila, we have a ringer. Meet the fake Jumpin'Jimmy. This horse can beat the nags he was racing against with only three legs. How they kept him under wraps is a trick only Butch will know. Well, I have the ringer identified, but unfortunately, he is dead. I am sure that the horse has disappeared, with the proof that I need. They used him to win a couple of million bucks, then killed him, son-of-a-bitches!

CHAPTER NINETEEN

These people will stop at nothing. The way that they achieve their objectives is ruthless. I remember the term that Doc used when he patched up Bret Jacobs, "devoid, void of any human feeling, never giving a thought to the welfare of another human being, and will use any means necessary to kill or harm a person without any remorse or worry about consequences." One of these people has to be responsible for carrying out the task. I suspect that Bruno follows the orders of the little old lady. Butch is the loudmouth front man, but he also takes orders from her. She must be clever enough to put the schemes together and set up the national wagering format. I have to get more information on Bruno. He probably isn't listed as an owner or groom, so Bill will have a difficult time in locating something on him. I spot Bill as he is walking out of the race office, no doubt speaking to the judges.

I tell him what I need and he says he'll get right on it. I tell him I don't have a last name, so it may take some time. He nods and is off. I see Jack Ballot, the rover, looking at us. Maybe Bill will check with him. I remember Bill telling me that Horseshoe was the contact who told him about the farm. I think 'shoe hasn't been quite as truthful as he should be considering I have a drug charge hanging over his black ass. I decide to look him up again. I drive by the blacksmith shop, but there is no movement. I proceed to the grooms' building, park, back in, and walk through the broken front door. Another pane is busted, I guess someone lost in that card game the other night. There is a rec room on the first floor with two beat up pool tables and a coke machine. Playing pool on one of the tables are a couple of sleazebags.

Neither of them acknowledges my presence. "I'm looking for Horseshoe. Anyone seen him lately?" I wait. I know I said it loud enough. "Excuse me, did anyone see Horseshoe?"

The bigger white guy answers as he shoots. "Nope." I feel I'm going to have a problem, so I plan a little ploy. I find the cell phone and speak in it.

"Good buddy, you can com'on. These are the guys you're looking for." The other little white guy stands straight up and stares at the big white guy.

"Who you callin' fella'. We ain't done nothin'."

"Well you can speak. If I don't get some info and fast, I'll call good buddy again and have them cuff your asses. They're looking for a twosome that robbed a store about one hour ago, and you guys fit the bill."

"We ain't robbed no store, mister. We ain't never left the grounds."

"Now. Let me try that again. Where's Horseshoe?"

The little guy answers for the scumbags. "He ain't been here all day. It's unusual, 'cause 'shoe, he ain't never miss a day." I don't like the tone of that at all.

The other white guy chimes in. "If'n you need to find him, I can send you to a place where he hangs. It ain't no place for a white guy, especially a white cop." I guess they aren't as dumb as they look.

"I'm listening."

"You know where the colored section of town is?" The big guy is in charge. I nod, knowing I don't have a clue. "Go to the Sapphire Lounge, you'll find him there." I thank them and leave, walking backwards all the way. As I start the Chevy, I call Bill on the cell phone and ask him where the Sapphire Lounge is. He gives me directions and asks if I need cover. I say no, but stay by the phone. He suggests I don't drive there but take a cab. I take the suggestion and have a cab pick me up at the guard shack. The old-timer on duty doesn't give it any thought, another cop. The cab is prompt. I get in and give him directions to the Sapphire Lounge. The cabby balks and turns around. I give him the directions, again, and this time I tell him to wait in front of the joint. The drive is a short one and I can see why the cabby was hesitant, the hood isn't in the best of shapes. It's a damn shame, but every city I go to has the same hood. Who says all Americans are equal? He drives down a side street and just ahead is a blue building with a large sign hanging from a shaky bar. The sign says "Sapphire Lounge". It is apparent that the lounge is segregated, that doesn't bother me. I can be such a naïve asshole at times. The cabby makes a U-turn and parks in the direction from which he came. I like this guy's style. I tell him to wait, he nods, and keeps the meter running. When I get out of the cab I hear the automatic door locks kick in. Now, I really like this guy. I smile at him and walk to the joint. I gaze through the window first to see if the big fella is here, a sea of black. I walk in. The noise level drops in half, with all eyes looking at me. I wave at everyone and say I'm just looking for someone, it doesn't work. A honey breaks from the crowd and strolls up.

"Dahlin', you in the wrong spot. You color blind or sumthin'?"

"No, sweetheart, I'm looking for someone. I'm from out of town and I'm not a cop. I have some business with a gentleman."

"Shit, dahlin', there ain't no gentleman in here. You sell drugs? The only time we see white folk here is if they are selling drugs or buying drugs. Now, who you lookin' for? Ole Mable can fix you up."

"Thanks for the help Mable, and I'm not buying or selling drugs. I'm looking for Horseshoe." The noise that wasn't quiet when I walked in is quiet now. The place is a damn morgue. Mable cocks her head.

"Honey, you strikin' out today. Ole 'shoe can't see you right now."

"Excuse me, you mean he's not here?" She nods. The place

is still quiet.

A voice from the back yells "He's a cop, Mable. Let's hang his ass." The place starts to stir again, and I'm the cause.

Mable takes charge, "now, wait a minute, fellas. Let's give Vanilla a chance to speak before ya'll do somethin' you regret. You got the floor, sugah'."

"Horseshoe and I had a deal going on. He asked me to meet him here. I'm only doing as I was asked to do. If you say he's not here, then that's good enough for me." I start to walk out but a black wall appears in front of the door.

"Not so fast, sugah. The boys don't quite believe you and neither do I. You gotta do better than that." Think fast, Domino! I decide to play a hunch.

"Old 'shoe called me and asked me to check into a man's death. He said one of your people has been done wrong." I got their attention.

"Keep talkin'." A deep voice speaks from the back of the crowd.

"Old 'shoe wanted to find out who killed Cotton." I wait, and pray. I hear murmurs, I think I got lucky.

"You got somethin' to do with those white folks at the track?" Another voice from the back emerges.

"Not really, but 'shoe knew me from another track and he thought I could help. We were going to meet tonight because he had some info for me." They start to get a little more restless.

Mable takes charge again. " I think Vanilla is tellin' the truth. If it's all right with you fellas, I'll fill him in on what happened. We all know Cotton shouldn't have got killed." There are moderate okays as she leads me to a table. I have to take a leak, but I'm gonna hold it.

"You took a big chance comin' in here fella. We aren't too happy because the white folk has killed Cotton and now 'shoe. You know where I'm comin' from?" I'm stunned, but nod. Lady, I know exactly where you are coming from.

"I'm listening." Mable cocks her head, again and speaks.

"Horseshoe was found early this morning stuffed in a dumpster not far from here. His was carved up like a Christmas turkey. The man who found him screamed, then passed out. Some of the neighbors came to his aid. We left the body in the dumpster.

Now it is my turn to cock my head. I look straight at her. She doesn't budge. We lock eyes for what seems like several minutes. I'm the first to move. I have to see the body, so I take another chance.

"Mable, will you take me to the body?" The head tilts again.

"If the boys find out you are a cop you won't leave here. They know all the town cops, so they could give a shit about an out of town cop. why should I help you?" That is a good question. There is absolutely no reason why this lady has to help me. I think fast.

"I'm not a cop cop, but a sort of cop. You know what I mean? I have been sent here to solve the crimes at the track, and 'shoe was a big help to me." We lock eyes again. I'm not going to budge this time. She does.

"Does anyone know you are here?"

"I have a cab waiting for me in front."

"Describe the cabby to me."

"He's a white guy, thirtyish, with short blond hair. He smells, too."

She smiles. "That's Edgar, he's a Polack, doesn't speak good English. I'll send him away." Before I can stop her, she hustles some guy over to the table and gives an order. "Benny, get a fifth of gin from the storeroom and give it to Eddie. He's outside in the cab waitin' for Vanilla here. Tell him Mable says it's okay and not to worry." Benny does what he is told. "I'll get you home, honey". I sure as shit hope so, honey. I follow her out the back door to an alley. She waves a finger and I follow. The woman has power.

I catch up to her. "How far?"

"Don't worry, sugah, as long as you are with me, you're okay."

The walk is a short one. Around a corner and down the block we go until we stop at a large blue dumpster in front of a tenement building. The building has seen better days. "This is it. I'll give you ten minutes with me here then we gotta go. Got it?" I nod.

I thought picking up a dead horse's head was bad enough, but this will surpass it. I climb in the dumpster and try not to look at all the blood. The body is slightly tilted so I can't move it, he's too heavy anyway. 'Shoe's ass is pointing towards me so his pockets are exposed. I feel in the left back pocket, the stench is becoming unbearable, nothing there. I feel in the right back pocket and find a key. I grab the key and climb out of the stench. I almost pass out when I hit the ground.

"You alright fella?" I nod, holding my self up against the dumpster.

"How am I going to get home?" She tilts her head and blinks.

"Come with me. I told the boys I'd be back in one hour. I own the joint and they know if I find anything out of whack, their asses are out the door. I service one of the Sheriff's boys, so they know I mean business." She smiles at that. "He's a white boy, too," No wonder she smiles. I follow her to an older Caddy, in good shape. She unlocks the doors and we climb in. The Caddy starts and we are driving out of this section. The windows are tinted so no one can see in, she thinks of everything. "Where to?"

"Drop me on the corner by the track. I'll walk from there." I see her nod.

She arrives at the spot. " I didn't see you and I don't wanna know your name. Got it Vanilla?" I nod, open the door and get out. Before I can say thank you, the door closes and the

Caddy flies up the street. At least she doesn't have to worry about getting any tickets. Before I hoof it the short distance to the track, I duck behind a tree and piss. It is almost nightfall, and the track seems quiet. I open the Chevy, start it, and drive to Bill's house. I was considering giving 'shoe some of the dirty money, but forget about that. Maybe, I'll go into business with Mable. I smile at the thought while I pull into the driveway fiddling with 'shoe's key in my hand.

Bill and the gals are finishing dinner when I waltz in. Bill and I catch eyes but don't speak. The girls say the obligatory hellos. I return the greetings and decline the meal Ellie has prepared. It is hard to pass up vegetable lasagna, fresh greens and a bottle of Chianti, but I don't have an appetite. I look at Bill and nod to the porch, ever so slightly, so as not to alarm the ladies. I stroll to the porch and light a cig. A few minutes pass until Bill joins me. I start from the beginning.

"Thanks for the directions, they are perfect. The cabby is apprehensive, but he drives me anyway. The place is not friendly, but some gal, Mable, gives me some slack. After some fencing with the crowd they believe me. Mable takes me to a table and explains that 'shoe is carved up and left in a dumpster. She shows me where he is. I climb in to look around, not a pleasant sight. I search his pockets and find a key. (I hold it up for him to see). She drives me to the corner and I walk to where the Chevy is parked. And here I am."

"Mable is a good person, she has connections." I nod remembering what Mable said about her squeeze. Bill continues. "You took a big chance, but you must have persuaded Mable with some smooth talk, or you wouldn't be here now. The town has a problem with white guys going there and selling drugs to these people, but Mable puts a stop to it. It's a segregated place, but they're all right. Mable has total control." Yeah, that woman has power, no doubt about that! Bill changes the conversation. "We have a lead on Bruno. The name we got from the FBI is Bruno Scippio. The description fits and his military records indicate his natural mother's name is Glenda, no last name given. I have got to figure it's the same Glenda we know. Sal, this man is heavily trained in Special Forces and spent time in the Gulf War. He knows everything from torture, self-defense, bomb making, weapons-a full arsenal. He tried one of his tactics on a CO, but it wasn't thought of as a kind gesture, so he was court-martialed in 1997. The CO filed civil charges against him. He disappeared and the military hasn't caught up to him yet, nor have any local authorities. I think this is our guy."

Now it is my turn to digest. I guess we know who has tortured these people, then killed them. The whole deal bothers me. How can two men and an older lady commit all of these crimes and orchestrate this scheme? There has to be someone else involved, someone who is close to the action and someone who knows my every step. I think back on the leak, maybe, just maybe, the leak is here at the track. It seems possible that someone has been playing me and these horsemen like a symphony. I have got to keep digging.

"Bill, what about this key. Can you figure where it fits?" I hand him the key and he rolls it around in his fingers.

"Sal, it looks like a key that may fit a locker at a bus or train station. I'll keep it and snoop around." I nod. I thank Bill for the info and retire to the shower. I've got to get that stenchy smell and feeling out of me. When I'm happy I usually warble in the shower, some nice smooth jazz stuff, but the vocal chords are giving way to my brain. I'm thinking. I'm deep in thought and don't hear Mary rummaging around in the room. I'm surprised when I step out of the shower, buck naked, and she's staring at me.

"Well, don't you look cute in your birthday suit."

"I didn't hear you, I was deep in thought. I'm trying to figure something out. Has the agency called the track trying to locate us?"

"I checked with the switchboard. There has been one message from Jack. The message was no big deal. They don't miss us Sal. If they knew the extent of this deal, they would pay closer attention to it. I know you don't want to tell them shit, so I didn't call them back."

"Good, I prefer that"

I have been ignoring the brewskis, so I pop a top and swig on one. It feels great and mellows me out some. She returns from the shower and we resume where we started a few nights ago. After making love we fall asleep in each other's arms.

CHAPTER TWENTY

I miss waking up next to a beautiful woman. I miss the touch, feel and smell of sex. I miss seeing a beautiful body parade around a room with no inhibitions at all. I miss seeing a woman naked after a shower. I miss a woman preparing herself for the day, making sure every little detail is the way she wants it. The act, performed with a genuine partner, makes the feeling indescribable. I have screwed up several relationships because of my insecurity, and I'll probably screw this one up again. When this case is over, I'll take on another, somewhere else in the country. I'll go through the same pain and frustration I always go through. Perhaps I am better off by myself. Mary and Gretchen, and to some extent, Susan have provided me with some confidence that I can return to being a normal man.

"Domino, Domino, Domino...?"

"I'm sorry Mary, I am thinking about something." I won't tell her that it is us that I'm thinking about, because I don't want to disappoint her again.

"Do you want me to follow up on the print-outs?"

"Yes, try and find out if there is a trail of cashed tickets somewhere in the United States. It is the law that if a person wins a certain amount he or she has to sign a 1099 winning form. Check with each state and find out their law and the amount. Ask the wagering outlet if they suspect a ten-per center (someone who signs for the real winner of a ticket and receives 10% for his trouble). The ten-per center will have to claim the winnings on their taxes, while the actual winner gets all the cash, less 10%, and doesn't report a thing. A lot of people make a good living ten-percenting.) If there are names, fax them to the Wagering facilitator's office. Also, work on some local banks and see if Glenda Jackson, Bruno Scippio, or Butch Green has opened a wire account. I doubt if the account will be local. Find out which Caribbean Islands handle such transfers. I know that is a lot to do, but we need more than speculation, we need more proof. Got it?"

She stares at me and doesn't answer.

"What's the matter, that's not a lot for you to do. As good as you are on the phone with people, you can obtain that info in a couple of days."

"You are going after them, aren't you?" The stare is fixed and cold.

"What makes you think I'm going to do that?"

"I know you Sal Domino. You have to do everything yourself. You go on this trip of yours and won't allow anyone to help because you feel that someone, other than yourself, is going to get hurt or killed." She's right. That is the reason no one will work with me and why I won't allow anyone to work with me. The tactics I use in the field are, at best, borderline, and I don't want anyone tagging along. I'll bust these guys my way. If I take a bullet, then I'm the only one that is in danger. Besides, after seventeen years, it has worked. I have enough balls and luck to pull it off, and I do.

"Yes, I am. I will tell Bill what I'm doing but I won't tell him any details. Mary, you know me better than anyone, I will not endanger another soul when the bust comes. I've put enough people in danger in this case, and my actions probably account for some of the deaths here. I have to do it my way, you know that."

Her stare isn't going away. "If that's the way you want it, fine. At least allow Bill to cover you some. I'll say a novena for you." She always says that, and you know what, they work. I'm still alive, between the novenas from my mother and Mary, I must be protected. "When are you going to notify Bill?"

"I'm going to meet him this afternoon to discuss a plan. Thanks for the support Mary, it means a lot to me. I will think about it when someone is shooting at my ass." I walk to her and peck the cheek, then walk to the kitchen where Ellie has the coffee ready. Bill has already left for the track. I will catch up with him about lunchtime. Maybe he has the info on the key I found in Horseshoe's jeans. I thank Ellie and unlock the Chevy. I haven't looked at the cash in awhile, so I peek under the seat and find it resting comfortably. What the hell am I going to do with that cash?

The Chevy starts, and I pull out of the driveway. The drive to the track is uneventful. The guard at the guard shack nods and I scoot through and navigate to Bill's office. The rover, Jack Ballot, waves as I pass him. He's the one who is supposed to have all the contacts in the barn area. I wonder if Bill uses him a lot? Bill sees me as I drive up.

"We have a lead on the key. I went to the bus station and talked to the supervisor and he said it isn't one of their keys, but possibly could be a train station key. The only problem is there isn't a train station for thirty miles. The closest one is Warren, north of here. I called the train station and spoke to a supervisor there. He asked me to describe the key and I did. He said it sounds like it could be theirs because of the markings on it. What do you think?" Good question, a damn good question.

"Did 'shoe own a car?"

Bill went into the office and returned with his parking roster. "No, he didn't even have a driver's license. The only ID I have for him is an old Social Security card."

"Did he have any other friends on the track that you know of, did he?"

Bill shakes his head. "Shoe was a loner, except when he went to Mable's. He stayed mostly on the track, hustling horseshoes."

"I have to drive to Warren, Bill. Cover me with anyone

that wants to find me." He nods and gives me the key. I swing by Gretchen's barn, just to say hi, and don't find her. I continue out, wave to the guard, and proceed to a gas station to fill the Chevy, and get cigs. The drive to Warren does not allow me to go by any more of the old stomping places. It's a boring drive on the thruway.

Before I know it I'm at the outskirts of Warren. The town is desolate and I can't figure why the train stops here. I know it used to be an old steel town, but those factories have been closed for several years. It seems all the mountains have seen their better days, including Warren. I stop next to a cop and ask directions to the train station, and receive them with a grin. I guess the crime rare in Warren isn't very big if a cop smiles at strangers. I drive a block, turn left and look to the right and find the station. I turn around and park the Chevy in the direction from which I came. I'm in a strange town, can't take any chances. I lock the Chevy and walk to the terminal. The place smells like an old train station, stale cigarettes and beer. Some weary travelers have spent many a lonely night in this place. There is only one man on duty.

"Is the supervisor around?" A middle aged, balding gent raises his head to speak, then changes his mind. Instead he nods his head to the left where an older man is sitting out of view of the public. The gent puts his head back down and pretends to work. I walk down to the hidden man.

"Hello, are you the supervisor?" He spotted me when I came in, so he is ready for some conversation.

"Yes, I'm Joe Gordan. Did you speak to me on the phone a little while ago, sonny?" Why do older people call younger males, sonny? I will be polite.

"Well, sort of. A colleague of mine spoke to you. Is this one of your keys?" I hold up the key, but don't give it to him. He looks at it.

"Do you mind if I check the serial number to make sure?" I hold the key and turn it so he can see the numbers. That seems to satisfy him. " Just a moment please while I check this," he continues. In a short while he returns with a puzzled expression on his face. He stares at me. "What are you doing with this key, sir?" He's a sharp old coot. I didn't figure they would follow procedures in this hick town. I guess I have to play along before I show some ID.

"This key is part of an investigation. Why do you ask?"

"The person that checked this locker out is a large black man, and you sir, are not a large black man." How observant of the old timer I say to myself, sarcastically. I pull the ID out and flash it. He takes it and reads it carefully, turning it over as if to check its authenticity. "Very well, sir, follow me." I always do what I'm told. He leads me to a shabby room with walls that are in need of paint. The room smells like stale piss as we head to the far end. Horseshoe's locker is the last one on the right. He waits for me to open it, I don't like that.

"Joe, I can handle it from here." I wait as the old man gives me a haughty look and walks away. I use the key to open the locker. The locker smells like the room. In it I see some news articles and pictures of 'shoe holding the reins of a horse, with Butch by his side. It was probably the highlight of this poor slob's career, a stupid picture in a newspaper. Next to the papers is a bag. Now I know there can't be any news in this thing. I lift and find it heavy. I've felt that kind of weight before. I reach inside and pull out money, lots of it. It seems as though Horseshoe wasn't totally candid with me after all. There's about ten thousand in the bag. I don't have time to mess with it, so I stuff the bag into my jacket, shut the locker and start to walk out. I wave at the two gentlemen, neither smile at me. I check both ways when I enter the street and proceed to the Chevy. I unlock it, put the stash next to the other stash and begin to drive away. The way out of town is simple. I'm thirsty so I pull in to a convenience store and grab a Pepsi. I don't take long, but just enough time for someone to mess with my Chevy. I leave the Chevy for one minute and someone messes with me. I start to rile the guy who is sitting in the front seat, but he turns to me and shows a gun that is much larger than my thirty-eight. I freeze. It's Jack Ballot, the rover, and he doesn't look friendly.

"Get in the car and shut up. Give me the gun and start driving out of town to Drawbridge, you know the way." I do as I am told.

CHAPTER TWENTY ONE

The first fifteen minutes are pure hell. I keep glancing to my right and see what looks like a forty-five. Forty-five is larger than thirty-eight anyway you slice it. Ballot keeps staring at me, not uttering a word. I decide to break the ice.

"So, Jack, how much are they paying you to pad their bank accounts? I hope it is plenty." He doesn't take his eyes off me but doesn't speak either. "What's the matter Jack, won't they let you speak?" He reaches over and swats my hand with that monster he is holding. I'm reduced to driving with one hand. "Com'on Jack, I'm just trying to make some conversation. You don't have to slug me. You didn't answer the question, how much?"

"None of your business, Domino. Keep driving before I forget they want you alive, for awhile." He grins, then shifts the monster to the other hand. I have to play it out and wait for a chance to escape.

"When did you learn that I was coming to Wildwood?" No answer, he is either afraid to talk or has been commanded not to talk. "You set all those people up to die Jack, you know that don't you?" He stirs, restlessly.

"Listen Domino, shut the hell up. I heard you are a pesky bastard with that mouth of yours. Leave it alone, I don't have anything to lose, I'm cooked already." He turns to look out the window. I almost have a chance there, but he recovers quickly. "Keep driving, asshole."

I let a few minutes pass then I start up again. "I can help you Jack. Is it worth going to the chair for a few bucks?"

"It's not a few bucks, Domino. These people have netted over $5 million in the three races so far. My cut is substantial.

There is a person like me at the other two tracks to make sure the plans are carried out, and to take care of business, if necessary. I didn't kill anyone, Domino. I may have set some people up, but I didn't kill anyone." He stops and ponders what he has told me. "Now, shut the hell up!" His tone seems irrational, so I behave.

"Alright Ballot, no more questions about the sting. But I'm curious about one thing." I wait for a reaction, don't get one, so I proceed. "I thought you are a retired cop. Bill speaks highly of you. Where did you go wrong, Jack?" I wait again, this time he is more restless than before. I think I'm getting to him.

"Man, you are a talkative son-of-a-bitch. Why should I answer questions for a man who is about to bite the bullet?" Good question. At least I know my fate, unless something drastic happens. I assume I'm going to meet Mom and the boys, how exciting.

"Exactly why you should answer the question, Jack, is if I'm toast anyway, what's the difference? I can't hurt anyone if I'm dead."

"Domino, you got balls, there isn't any doubt about that! I read with interest the case you solved at a dog track where you impersonated a trainer. You set those guys up, big time." "If you must know, I was a cop but was terminated because I was on the take. Cop pay in Montana isn't much, so these lottery people came in and wanted a front man to hide what they were doing, and I fit the bill. Beane doesn't know about that, because I turned state's evidence and they expunged my records. I've always had larceny in my blood, especially when I can make a good score."

I listen carefully to his tale. A bad cop, a really bad cop. Just as in racing, a few bad ones make it tough for the legitimate ones. I can't get to this guy, so I'm better off keeping quiet for the time being. We are approaching Drawbridge. I drive slowly over the rickety bridge and follow the same road

I was on before. This time I don't stop and hide the car as before, we drive right through the open gate to the trailer.

"Pull around back. I don't want anyone to see your car." I do as I'm told. I put the Chevy in park and turn to him. Should I offer him the stash I have under the seat? I think otherwise and stare at him. "Keep the seat belt on until I come around to your side" I watch him as he gets out of the car and walk to my side. He opens the door, unlocks the belt, and pulls me out.

"Ballot, I'm not helpless!" My tone is a little rattled. I hope he doesn't pick up on it. I have to remain cool, so I swagger to the trailer. A voice rings out. "Over here Ballot, in the barn." It's the old lady. Should I call her Glenda or wait to be introduced. The monster gun prods me towards the barn.

"Well, well sonny boy. It's so good to see you again." "Did he give you any problem, Jack?" Jack shakes his head. "Good boy, Sal. You know I was married to a good Italian fella once, name was Scippio. I guess you know that by now, huh. We were stealing social security checks and he got a little greedy. I dumped him in Texas somewhere, haven't seen him since. Of course the place I dumped him was the desert. I wonder if he made it out? Oh well, to the task at hand."

She is the most conniving, unscrupulous bitch, I have come across in all my years of fighting crime. She has no conscience.

"You know Sal, you should cover your tracks better. Jack figured you would find out about the locker sooner or later, so he kept watching you. When you made the trip Jack was right behind you. Now you are mine. If I know your methods, you didn't tell anyone where you went because the great Domino likes to work alone. Tsk,tsk, Sal, bad boy." She paces the stall we are in. My ass is grass and she is the lawnmower. If I get out of this alive, I'll be very fortunate. I keep thinking while she broods. "Bruno will love to meet you, Sal. He has practiced on a whole bunch of people. I think he will do something different to you. Of course, no one will ever find your body." I decide to try and rattle her. Shit, what's the difference if they kill me now or Bruno does his thing on me later.

"Glenda, why don't we make a deal. Jack tells me that you have a person like him at the other tracks." The old lady turns to Jack and gives him a stare that turns my stomach. Obviously, Jack talks too much. I got to keep at her. "I can be the go between in the cases and cover all the tracks, and still look like I'm doing a great job. The only difference is, I won't solve the cases. I'll go on a few cases and won't solve them, then with the money you give me I'll retire in Aruba or some tropical island and you won't hear from me again. How's that sound?"

"Don't listen to him, Glenda. He's a talker, just full of shit."

"Shut up Jack! It appears you had a conversation with him on the way up here. How do I know you didn't spill all the beans to him?" She glares at Jack. The crooked cop is shaken.

"What's the difference. He's gonna die anyway. Don't listen to his shit. He's trying to get in your head." Jack's pleading won't work.

"Maybe I should use him. He has more sense than you do. At least he won't run his mouth to the wrong people. Why did you have to talk to him? I told you to get his ass and drive him to me. That's all I said." She reaches around to her back and whips out a twenty-two, one of those snub nose jobs that issues hollow points. It will kill, make no mistake about that. I have succeeded in riling her, but I'm not ready for what happens next. She points the twenty-two at Jack's head and pulls the trigger. Jack drops like melted butter, one clean shot to the forehead. The shot startles me, and I jump back. She immediately points the gun at me. I raise my hands again and stare at the smoke oozing out of the barrel. No sir, my ass is staying put. The shot brings people from the mobile home. The two sons arrive, Butch and Bruno, frick and frack.

Butch is the first to enter the barn, "Momma, what's the matter? We heard shots." Butch stops because Jack Ballot's body is sprawled across the entrance. The boys look at each other in

astonishment.

"Bruno, take this piece of shit to the lake and dump him. Be sure he is weighted down. Go help him Butch, I'll be all right with the fast talker here. He ain't movin' for shit." She's right about that. The boys do as they are told. Butch gets a wheelbarrow and Bruno lifts the body up and gets him in. They move off quietly. The bitch and I are face to face.

"You want to try anything, Domino? That was a good trick you pulled on Jack. You got him to talk. What else did he say before his untimely demise?" Her look says it all. I'll feed her some more shit.

"Small talk, really. He described his cop life. I guess he was lonely for someone to talk too. I was just killing time until we arrived here." She roars at my statement. What the hell is so funny, I was telling the truth!

"Domino, you are a piece of work! The boys say you have a lot of balls. Boy, you are a piece of work!" Her tone changes from laughing to serious in the flash of an eyelash. " What do you want me to do with you now, Sal. I can't let you go, you saw me kill Ballot. I'm afraid this will have to be the end. Boy, I could use a guy like you." She raises the gun and points to my head. I'm looking at an empty barrel, soon to be filled with a bullet for me.

"We're done Ma." The boys enter from behind her. She makes the fatal mistake of turning her head to look at them. I have my chance. I knock her gun in the air and push her towards the boys. I catch the gun before it hits the floor and run down the barn aisle toward the other end. Of course, if either of the boys has a gun, I'm dead. The stupid idiots tend to their mother instead of chasing me. She yells to them to get me and leave her alone. I have a fifty-foot head start. I figure I can outrun Bruno, but not Butch, he's in shape. I fly out the other end and head for open pasture. There is a tractor about one hundred feet from me. Just as I figure, Butch is leading the chase. He fires two shots at me and both miss to my right, hitting the ground. Bruno is lagging behind with his gun drawn. The old bitch is watching from the barn.

"Get his dago ass. Don't shoot him. Bring him to me, I want to kill him myself." Glenda can be heard in Wildwood. I hope someone close by hears her too.

I reach the tractor with Butch in hot pursuit. I crouch behind the wheel and take aim. The twenty-two isn't good at long distances, but at short range it can be a monster. I have to be patient. Butch is closing in, I aim, then squeeze the trigger. Bingo! I hit his leg and he falls, yelling in pain. Bruno is way behind, but I don't want to engage him, so I make a beeline to a lean-to in the pasture next to me. I hear Bruno shouting, "Butch is hit, Ma. He's hurt real bad." Bruno starts to lift Butch and bring him to the barn when the old lady yells, "Leave his ass, get Domino. He won't bleed to death. Get Domino!" Her voice is penetrating and strong. Now I know where Butch gets his mouth from. While they are talking I move to the lean-to. Bruno sees me, but is cautious. He has seen his brother get shot, and he doesn't want the same. He crouches behind the tractor and looks my way.

"Hey, Domino. You can't hide from me. I'll get you sooner or later. And when I do, I'll carve you up, real pretty like. Then I'll drop you off to that pretty Gretchen girl and let her see you. Yeah, I like that plan. Watch out, Domino, I'm coming." He starts to move. It is too far for me to shoot, besides, I need the bullets. Instead, I'll mess with his head a little.

"Hey, Bruno. You're too stupid to do anything. You don't have the sense your mother gave you. How did you come out of that bitch anyway? You're too ugly to be a baby." Those are my best shots. I told you my methods would not make a training manual. But the assholes that write those manuals aren't in the field getting shot at like me.

"Domino, you shouldn't talk about my Ma that way. That is disrespectful. I'm gonna have a ball when I get you."

Glenda is hearing all this. "Stop bullshitting with him, Bruno. Just get his ass!" Bruno listens to the old lady, because I don't hear a peep. I look around and see a ditch about twenty feet behind me. The lean-to will cover me as I slip into the ditch. I can make my way back to the barn and surprise the old lady. It's a long shot, but I can't stay in the open field too long. I make my move. It has become very quiet. I can hear Bruno laboring as he approaches the lean-to, but I'm long gone. The ditch is half full of muddy water. I step gingerly, watching my feet. I crouch so Bruno can't see me. I move about one hundred feet, then turn around to look for Bruno and he isn't there. Can he be ahead of me? Butch isn't by the tractor, either. He probably limped his way to the barn. I don't see Bruno anywhere. It's decision time. Do I continue and get trapped at the barn or double back to the lean-to and hope I don't run into Bruno. I opt for the latter. I retrace my steps in the ditch until I reach the lean-to. Dusk is approaching. I catch my breath. Bruno isn't here, or at the tractor. I can only surmise he went back to the barn to meet with the old lady. I relax for a second then I hear him from the back of the lean-to.

"Where ya' goin' Domino?" He lunges for me and knocks the gun out of my hand. He picks me up and slams me into the side of the lean-to. I'm hurting all over. He reaches for me and I kick him in the balls. He buckles and yells some words I can't understand. The words sure aren't Italian. I try to run but he grabs my leg. I kick him in the face with my free leg and break away. I look back and see he is slow to get up. I decide to be offensive. I run to him and kick his face again. I kick his kidneys, twice. The big man is groaning and writhing in pain. Special forces, my ass. I kick him until he no longer moves. I catch myself. I keep kicking him until I'm tired. I'm exhaust-

ed. I feel for a pulse, and get one. He won't be going anywhere for a long time. I get my gun and tuck it in my pants. I
will use his Berretta, if I need to. The Beretta fits my hand
nicely. I start to walk to the barn looking for the old lady and
Butch. They don't know what has happened to the brute and
won't expect me. I duck down as I reach the barn. I do not
hear voices. As I move to the trailer, I hear the high-pitched
tone of Butch.

"Damn, Ma, it hurts. Take it easy."

"Stop your whining, I got to stop the bleeding. I underestimated Domino, he is a tricky bastard, a worthy opponent."

"What do you mean opponent. This isn't basketball, ma.
This guy is going to send us to the chair if we don't get him."
You're right Butch, I'm gonna get ya'.

"Bruno will get him, Butch. Don't worry about it."

"Bruno won't be going anywhere for awhile." I step in the
door and point the Beratta at the old lady. They look at me as
if I have risen from the dead. "What's the matter, you see a
ghost?"

"What have you done with Bruno. You killed him, didn't
you? You bastard, you killed my baby." She rushes for me and
I cuff her in the jaw. Down she goes. Butch tries to get up and
I wave the Beratta at him.

"Not a good idea, Butch. I would love to shoot your loud-
mouthed ass, but I need you for the DA." I guess he didn't
want to listen, because he got up and limped toward me. His
actions are fast and I duck just at the right moment. A knife
swooshes by my head, then another hits my shoulder. Where
did they come from? I fall on top of the old lady and he
makes another move at me. I lose the Beratta in the fall, so I
reach for the twenty-two and find it. I aim and shoot Butch
twice in the stomach at close range. He falls on top of the old
lady and me. I have a devil of a time excavating myself from
that mess. I pull the knife from my shoulder and scream. I'll
stuff a towel in the wound until help arrives. The old lady is

groggy, so with one hand I tie her up. I make sure she isn't going anywhere. Butch is dead. I cover him with a blanket from the bedroom. I sit with my head down, totally exhausted and hurt. I reach for the cell phone and hope it works. It does and I call Bill. He answers at home. "Bill, send the cops and an ambulance to the farm in Drawbdidge. I'll wait" I pass out.

CHAPTER TWENTY TWO

Bill arrives.......

"Sal, are you awake. Sal, talk to me."

I'm groggy, but I hear voices. I open my eyes and recognize Bill. He is fuzzy, I think it is him, I'm not sure. " Is that you Bill?" I'm fading again. I hear muffled voices, a lot of them. Are Ma and the boys still alive? Are they going to kill me? I scream, loud and long. Who are the voices? I think I hear Bill. What the hell is happening to me?

Bill yells to the medics, "He's delirious. We have to get him to a hospital." Bill looks at the scene. It must have been quite a showdown. Sal is lucky to be alive. But, that is his way, doing it by himself. Bill is working with the local authorities from the Sheriff's office. One of the deputies calls from the lean-to. As Bill walks in that direction he sees several deputies milling around. He enters the lean-to and sees what they are looking at. On the ground he sees the body of a large man. He is swollen beyond recognition and dead.

The lead Sergeant speaks for the men. "Did your man do this, Beane? If he did, he is a crazy son-of-a-bitch. What pissed him off enough to do this to a man?" Bill nods and walks away. Those deputies didn't see the bodies we have seen over the last two weeks. If they saw how they were carved and twisted up, maybe they would have second thoughts on the criticism. Bill had asked Mary to stay in Ellie's Caddy while Bill surveys the scene. He is walking back to the car thinking how he is going to explain the showdown.

"Tell me the truth, Bill. Is he still alive? Tell me Bill, "begs Mary.

"Yes, he's alive Mary. He is hurt and slightly delirious, but he will live. They are taking him to County Hospital. The two brothers are dead, but the old lady is alive. The Sheriff's men will take her into custody and file charges against her. When Sal is strong enough, he will have to furnish details about the crimes. Let's go home, we can't do anything else here."

"Can I see him Bill, just a glimpse?"

"No sweetheart, allow the medical people to do their thing. We'll catch up to him at the hospital. Let's go home Mary. We'll say a novena with dinner to help pull him through. Okay?" Mary nods.

Several hours later.......

Damn, I hurt all over. I bet I cracked those damn ribs again. I have to play the mummy routine again. As hard as I landed against the lean-to, it's a wonder I'm still in one piece. I guess adrenaline kept me going until the event was over. I don't remember much after that. I don't remember shooting the little rat, but I do remember cuffing the old lady. That felt good! I wonder if the oaf made it? I'll ask Bill when I see him. There is a nice hole in my shoulder, courtesy of Butch. I still don't know how he tossed those knives. I feel drowsy. I bet those nurses gave me some sedatives to make me sleep. It's working, I'm fading.

A few more hours pass........

Bill, Ellie and Mary enter the room. "Is he awake? Let's be quiet. I think I see some movement," says Mary. Sal's eyes open ever so slightly. When he focuses in on the faces he flashes a smile.

"It's about time you guys showed up. A man can die in these places without the proper TLC. Am I gonna live Bill?" Sal Domino, always the wise ass.

"Shit, you're too ornery to die. You are going to be fine. You have a nice hole in your shoulder, and your ribs are cracked again, but you'll make it. The agency will have you on another case in a couple of weeks."

Mary starts fussing, "Sal, I ought to kick your ass. Why didn't you call for back-up?" I guess some things will never change.

"I got jumped, Mary. I can make mistakes from time to time. Can Bill and I have a few moments alone? Nothing personal ladies, but I have to fill Bill in on a detail and it is confidential to the case." They look to each other and shrug their shoulders. It's a cop thing and they know not to take offense.

"Sit down Bill. I have to tell you something that you will not be pleased about." He looks at me as if the medication is going wacky on me, but complies anyway. I continue. "I found the train station and the locker easy enough, but I had a visitor when I was leaving the town. Jack Ballot was waiting for me. He gets the drop on me and escorts us to the farm in Drawbridge." The shock spreads across his face like a wildfire. His brows lift several times, and his nose twitches. I know he is trying to think how and when this all happened without me telling him, but it is no use. The case is so complex. He nods at me to continue, I do. " Somehow the old lady knew about Jack's past and recruited him. Jack took care of all the business on track that related to strong-arming, messages and surveillance on us. He was the leak, Bill. He knew when I was arriving, and every move thereafter. He signaled the old lady and she sent Bruno after the people who didn't comply, including yours truly. She actually thought I would leave the area and not try and solve the case. That way, she wouldn't have a fed murder on her hand. They became desperate when they saw I was not going anywhere, so they set a trap. You know the rest." I wait for him to settle down. One thing you don't do to a cop is push him. He will talk when he is ready. The Jack Ballot fact was upsetting to Bill. A good cop thinks he is a good judge of character, and when something fails, the cop takes it personally. I know the feeling.

"Where is he Sal? We've got to turn him on as an accesso-